PLOUGHSHARES

Spring 2008 · Vol. 34, No. 1

GUEST EDITOR
B. H. Fairchild

INTERIM EDITOR-IN-CHIEF
DeWitt Henry

MANAGING DIRECTOR
Robert Arnold

FICTION EDITOR
Margot Livesey

POETRY EDITOR
John Skoyles

ASSOCIATE FICTION EDITOR
Maryanne O'Hara

FOUNDING PUBLISHER
Peter O'Malley

ADVISORY EDITORS

Sherman Alexie
Russell Banks
Andrea Barrett
Charles Baxter
Ann Beattie
Madison Smartt Bell
Anne Bernays
Frank Bidart
Amy Bloom
Robert Boswell
Henry Bromell
Rosellen Brown
Ron Carlson
James Carroll
David Daniel
Madeline DeFrees
Mark Doty
Rita Dove
Stuart Dybek
Cornelius Eady
Martín Espada
Carolyn Forché
Richard Ford
George Garrett
Lorrie Goldensohn
Mary Gordon
Jorie Graham
David Gullette
Marilyn Hacker

Donald Hall
Joy Harjo
Stratis Haviaras
DeWitt Henry
Edward Hirsch
Jane Hirshfield
Alice Hoffman
Fanny Howe
Marie Howe
Gish Jen
Justin Kaplan
Bill Knott
Yusef Komunyakaa
Maxine Kumin
Don Lee
Philip Levine
Margot Livesey
Thomas Lux
Gail Mazur
Campbell McGrath
Heather McHugh
James Alan McPherson
Sue Miller
Lorrie Moore
Paul Muldoon
Antonya Nelson
Jay Neugeboren
Howard Norman
Tim O'Brien

Joyce Peseroff
Carl Phillips
Jayne Anne Phillips
Robert Pinsky
Alberto Ríos
Lloyd Schwartz
Jane Shore
Charles Simic
Gary Soto
Elizabeth Spires
David St. John
Maura Stanton
Gerald Stern
Mark Strand
Christopher Tilghman
Richard Tillinghast
Chase Twichell
Fred Viebahn
Ellen Bryant Voigt
Dan Wakefield
Derek Walcott
Rosanna Warren
Alan Williamson
Tobias Wolff
C. D. Wright
Al Young
Kevin Young

PLOUGHSHARES, a journal of new writing, is guest-edited serially by prominent writers who explore different and personal visions, aesthetics, and literary circles. PLOUGHSHARES is published in April, August, and December at Emerson College, 120 Boylston Street, Boston, MA 02116-4624. Telephone: (617) 824-8753. Web address: pshares.org.

ASSISTANT EDITOR: Laura van den Berg. EDITORIAL ASSISTANTS: Grace Schauer, Kat Setzer, and Jonathan Lazzara. HEAD READER: Jay Baron Nicorvo. PROOFREADER: Megan Weireter.

POETRY READERS: Simeon Berry, Jennifer Kohl, Grace Schauer, Kathleen Rooney, Heather Madden, Elisa Gabbert, Matt Summers, Autumn McClintock, Liz Bury, David Semanki, Chris Tonelli, Julia Story, Maria Halovanic, Pepe Abola, and Meredith Devney. FICTION READERS: Kat Setzer, Matt Salesses, Kathleen Rooney, Simeon Berry, Kat Gonso, Chris Helmuth, Leslie Busler, Jim Scott, Chip Cheek, Cam Terwilliger, Laura van den Berg, Sage Marsters, Eson Kim, Vanessa Carlisle, Brenda Pike, Wendy Wunder, Shannon Derby, Dan Medeiros, Sara Whittleton, Patricia Reed, Leslie Cauldwell, and Gregg Rosenblum. NONFICTION READER: Katherine Newman.

SUBSCRIPTIONS (ISSN 0048-4474): $24 for one year (3 issues), $46 for two years (6 issues); $27 a year for institutions. Add $12 a year for international ($10 for Canada).

UPCOMING: Fall 2008, a fiction issue edited by James Alan McPherson, will appear in August 2008. Winter 2008–09, a poetry and fiction issue edited by Jean Valentine, will appear in December 2008.

SUBMISSIONS: Reading period is from August 1 to March 31 (postmark and online dates). All submissions sent from April to July are returned unread. Please see page xxx for editorial and submission policies.

Back-issue, classroom-adoption, and bulk orders may be placed directly through PLOUGHSHARES. Microfilms of back issues may be obtained from University Microfilms. PLOUGHSHARES is also available as CD-ROM and full-text products from EBSCO, H.W. Wilson, ProQuest, and the Gale Group. Indexed in M.L.A. Bibliography, American Humanities Index, Index of American Periodical Verse, Book Review Index. Full publisher's index is online at pshares.org. The views and opinions expressed in this journal are solely those of the authors. All rights for individual works revert to the authors upon publication. PLOUGHSHARES receives support from the National Endowment for the Arts and the Massachusetts Cultural Council.

Retail distribution by Ingram Periodicals and Source Interlink. Printed in the U.S.A. by Edwards Brothers.

© 2008 by Emerson College   ISBN 978-1-933058-09-2

CONTENTS

Spring 2008

INTRODUCTION
B. H. Fairchild — 7

FICTION
Barbara Dimmick, *Honeymoon* — 46
Christie Hodgen, *Tom & Jerry* — 68
William Lychack, *Stolpestad* — 105
Maile Meloy, *Agustín* — 125
Gerald Shapiro, *Mandelbaum, the Criminal* — 153

NONFICTION
James Brown, *Missing the Dead* — 22
Alexis Wiggins, *Unanimal* — 180

POETRY
Betty Adcock, *Roustabout* — 11
William Baer, *Motes* — 13
   The Puzzle House — 14
Christopher Bakken, *Drunk* — 15
George Bilgere, *Muscle* — 17
Michelle Boisseau, *Eighteenth-Century Boisseau House* — 18
   Monstrance — 19
Bruce Bond, *Ringtone* — 20
Elizabeth Bradfield, *Phrenology* — 21
Robert Cording, *Gift* — 32
Chad Davidson, *Labor Days* — 34
Stephen Dunn, *Aesthete* — 36
   To a Friend Accused of a Crime He May Have Committed — 37
Peter Everwine, *Rain* — 39
Gary Fincke, *The Art of Moulage* — 40
Gregory Fraser, *Silverfish* — 42
Carol Frost, *Apiary XV* — 44
   Two Songs for Dementia — 45

Allen Grossman, *The Garden Oak*	54
R. S. Gwynn, *Body Politic*	56
Rachel Hadas, *Leaning In*	59
Tu Ne Quaesieris	61
Mary Stewart Hammond, *Facing Eternity*	62
Portrait of My Husband Reading Henry James	63
Sarah Hannah, *Some Pacific Vapor*	65
C. G. Hanzlicek, *Dolphin Weather*	66
Bob Hicok, *My Stab at Recruiting*	92
Tony Hoagland, *Powers*	94
Colette Inez, *Looking for Nana in Virginia*	96
What the Air Takes Away	97
Roy Jacobstein, *Black*	98
Mark Jarman, *Fates at Baptist Hospital*	99
Haiku	101
Ted Kooser, *110th Birthday*	102
Theater Curtains	103
Writing Paper	104
Jeffrey Levine, *A Slight Illumination, a Pacific Vapor*	112
David Mason, *From the Anthology*	113
Michael Meyerhofer, *The Clay-Shaper's Husband*	115
Robert Mezey, *Long Lines, Beginning with a Line Spoken in a Dream*	117
The Other Tiger	118
D. Nurkse, *Altamira*	120
Bertrand de Born Smuggles a Letter Out of Hell	121
Alicia Ostriker, *The Husband*	123
Winter Trees	124
Alison Pelegrin, *Tabasco in Space*	138
Catherine Pierce, *The Books Fill Her Apartment Like Birds*	141
A Short Biography of the American People by City	142
Ron Rash, *Dylan Thomas*	144
Shelton Laurel: 2006	145
Jay Rogoff, *Manhattan*	146
Clare Rossini, *After a Woodcut of a Medieval Anatomy*	147
Faith Shearin, *Each Apple*	149
Trees	150
Maurya Simon, *St. Jerome the Hermit*	151
Julie Suk, *Flying Through World War I*	182
Anne-Marie Thompson, *Babcia*	184

David Tucker, *The House*   185
Charles Harper Webb, *Three Abominations*   186
    What Kitty Knows   187
Alan Williamson, *For My Mother*   189
Irene Willis, *You Want It?*   191

ABOUT B. H. FAIRCHILD   *A Profile by Rebecca Morgan Frank*   192

BOOKSHELF / EDITORS' SHELF   198

CONTRIBUTORS' NOTES   7

Cover art:
2213 by
Pete Shelby
Oil on canvas, 36″ x 60″, 2007

Ploughshares Patrons

This nonprofit publication would not be possible without the support of our readers and the generosity of the following individuals and organizations.

COUNCIL
William H. Berman
Denise and Mel Cohen
Robert E. Courtemanche
Jacqueline Liebergott
Fannette H. Sawyer Fund
Turow Foundation
Eugenia Gladstone Vogel
Marillyn Zacharis

PATRONS
Audrey Taylor Gonzalez
Drs. Jay and Mary Anne Jackson
Alice Munro
Joanne Randall, in memory of
James Randall

FRIENDS
Jorie Hofstra
Tom Jenks and Carol Edgarian

ORGANIZATIONS
Bank of America
Emerson College
Houghton Mifflin
Massachusetts Cultural Council
National Endowment for the Arts

COUNCIL: $3,000 for two lifetime subscriptions and acknowledgement in the journal for three years.
PATRON: $1,000 for a lifetime subscription and acknowledgement in the journal for two years.
FRIEND: $500 for a lifetime subscription and acknowledgement in the journal for one year.

B. H. FAIRCHILD

Introduction

Running throughout this issue, though not by editorial design, is that typically postmodern sense of absence, in so many configurations: in the memoir, for instance, as loss; or in fiction, as the absence of fulfilled desire, the basic plot of a story being that someone wants something and has problems getting it; or in poetry, as the kind of absence that is also presence—what is not said, what cannot be said, but which haunts or illumines or in some way alters what is otherwise explicit. No doubt I am noticing this because my obsession these days is a certain kind of absence that is sociological and political but has everything to do with literature: the death of hundreds of small towns throughout the midwest, the vanishing of an entire stratum of American culture that produced the Willa Cathers, Sherwood Andersons, William Staffords, and Angie Debos of our world, as well as some of the writers in this issue—

*

The Beauty of Abandoned Towns

Finally we sold out—you know, the big farm eats the small farm.
—Edna Pforr, Hamberg, North Dakota

...ruins do not speak; we speak for them.
—Christoper Woodward, *In Ruins*

Jefferson, Marx, and Jesus. Looking back, you can hardly believe it.

Bindweed and crabgrass shouldering through asphalt cracks, rats scuttling down drainpipes, undergrowth seething with grasshoppers.

The bumper crop in 1929. I stood on the front porch, dawn rolling over me like a river baptism because I was a new man in a new world, a stand of gold and green stretching from my hands to the sun coming up. In a way, a mirage. We bought a house in town. There it is. Or was.

The water tower, taller than the copper domes of Sacred Heart in Leoville, silhouette flooding the football field, missing boards of the scavenged bleachers, minor prophecies: *Bobby + Pam forever, Panthers rule, peace now.*

Presence is absence, says the philosopher. The past devours the future. Look at the goatgrass and ragweed claiming the feed store.

Sunflowers banging their heads on a conclusion of brick, the wind's last argument lost in a yellow cloud.

Eugene Debs set up The People's College in Fort Scott. Meridel LeSeuer grew up there. It lasted three years. Imagine: Comrade Debs, Comrade Sheppard, Comrade LeSeuer. In Kansas.

The open windows of the high school no longer surprise, pigeons flying in and out, the dumb cry of blackboards, wooden desks hauled away with the carved names of the long absent, the lost, the dead, the escaped.

The Farmer's Alliance tried. Socialist farm policy was for them a straight road to Jefferson's democracy. But they were always blocked by the big landowners. The deal-breaker was profits, not politics. The harvest was top soil, not wheat.

The last hitching post. The last horse, I suppose. Like Sunday morning, the last hymn, the last person to hear the last hymn. *May the circle be unbroken.* The circle is broken.

We subscribed to the Haldeman-Julius Appeal to Reason, *published out of little Girard, Kansas. Our children grew up on his Little Blue Books. The Federalist Papers, Thoreau, Emerson, Marx, Ingersoll, Upton Sinclair.*

The clapboard stores, slats long ago sand-blasted in dust storms, bleached or ochre now, gray, the faint green and yellow of a Lipton Tea ad on red brick. Broken windows flashing the setting sun in a little apocalypse of light, blind men in shades staring at the horizon, waiting for a sign. Stillness everywhere.

You know, you're wasting your time. No one gives a shit about this. None of it. No one.

Dearth of cars, motion, grind of gears, noise of commerce, chatter and cry of farm kids dangling from the beds of rusted-out pickups, murmur and guffaw of old men outside the Savings and Loan, stories, jokes. Quiet as a first snow. Somewhere a dog barks. A wire gate slams shut.

I'm so goddamned old I still tense up when an afternoon sky darkens. A roller would come in, dust up to eight thousand feet. If you were in the field, you were lost until it cleared. Or dead from suffocation. Where was your family? Where were your children?

Houses with tin roofs, wrap-around porches for watching thunderstorms, most vacant, but here and there pickup windows flaming in sunset, trimmed lawn, history in forty years of license plates nailed to the garage wall. Cellar door. Swing set, that little violin screech of rusted chains, hush of evening, choir of cicadas. The living among the dead.

It started when agriculture professors began to teach farming as a business rather than a vocation. And then the big ones over the years ate the little ones. But in this country vocations are exploited. Ask the public school teachers.

The lords of grain: two cats fat on field mice lounge beneath the elevator steps where dust from a caleche road powders them white—wraiths, ghost-cats. Survivors.

On the other hand, subsidies kill small farms these days. But back then we were desperate. Our children were hungry. FDR kept us alive. Then something went wrong. Big got bigger, small died. Still dying, hanging on but bed-ridden. The Ogallala aquifer's almost tapped out. I mean, for God's sake.

Between the boarded bank and the welding shop husks drift like molted feathers or the sloughed scales of cottonmouths. Weeds waist-high shade the odd shoe still laced, a Coke carton bleeding into bluestem, dulled scraps of newsprint that say who died in Ashland or Sublette or Medicine Lodge.

It goes back to the oikos, *the Greek family farm. Some ethic, some code of honor, kept them small. Big was vulgar, immoral. The Romans, too. Cato the elder, rich as Joe Kennedy, taught his son agronomy, not commerce.*

They are not haunted. They are not the "ghosts of themselves." They are cousin to vanishing, to disappearance. They are the highway that runs through them.

The picture show shut down decades ago. That's where we saw the world, the world our children and grandchildren ran off to. What happens when a nation loses its agrarian populace? My grandson worked as an usher there. He's a poet now. We have more poets than farmers. I don't think that's what Jefferson had in mind.

Not even decline, but the dawn of absence. Architecture of the dead. The lives they housed are dust, the wind never stops.

Sixty percent of the American soldiers killed in Iraq are from small rural towns. The farmer/soldier, foundation of the Greek polis. *Fodder for war. Blood harvest.*

The wind never stops. *Our children were hungry.* The highway's long blade under the sun. *Something went wrong.* The towns are empty. *The circle is broken.*

BETTY ADCOCK

Roustabout

I was twenty-two, pretty maybe. It was a small town
county fair: hot dogs, freak show, cotton candy,
and heavy wheels laden with light,
all tuned to the gaudy air.

The Octopus—remember that one? Eight
arms like extended girders, the thing was a metal
Shiva juggling worlds: a cup spun at the end
of each madly oscillating arm, every cup
overfull of squealing kids or lovers drunk
on the whip-sharp unexpected torque
toward the expected rapture.

He was maybe twenty, bare-chested, tanned
and gleaming in the southern September night,
a kind of summer in the lights that played
across him as he pulled levers set to arm
the bright contraption with speed and plunge,
with whirl and rise. His hair was almost red
in the lights' translation. Not many
riders yet, when suddenly he leapt
onto one of the metal arms in its low sweep
and rose with it. And laughed.

I thought it might be for me, this showing
off. He jumped onto the next arm as it rose,
went up with it, then landed easy on the ground.
He vaulted the lowered ones as they went by,
stepped up again, and down again, then ducked
under so a steel arm grazed his cap. How long
ago it was.
        How long did I stand and watch

that wild control before I turned
to find my husband and child?

He's likely dead now, or deep asleep
in some wine-dark room, some ragged dream.
I think no golden years follow that life,
though I can still see him shining new
against black sky and turning stars—
chancing it, taking on the monster,
winning, dancing it.

Motes

He lies as still as possible and waits,
then opens up his eyes. They're everywhere.
Millions, billions of motes, dead as the fates,
hovering in the shafts of the morning air.
Detritus of the universe, debris,
the cosmic dust, polluted, dying, and dead,
an endless sinking suffocating sea
of sunlit dust that pins him to his bed.
He struggles not to breathe, to somehow withstand
their deadly assault into his lungs. He tries
to pay no notice as they softly land,
one by one, on the surface of his eyes.
Then he watches one come down. It hovers and floats.
But he can't close his eyes, they're clogged with motes.

The Puzzle House

"I think you think I don't know who you are,"
she says at the window, "but I know what I know."
She sits across her tiny, white, bizarre,
and sterile room, watching the falling snow.
He stares at the half-done puzzle on the floor:
Escher's *Waterfall*, just more confusions
for someone seldom coherent anymore,
being "aphasic" with monothematic delusions.
But now the stabilizers, clozapine,
and stimulants ignite some hope. She tries
to peer beyond the smothering routine:
"It's like a puzzle!" She looks into his eyes,
but fails. She doesn't have a clue:
"Where do you fit in? Which piece are you?"

CHRISTOPHER BAKKEN

Drunk

When William Blake came fashionably late
to parties he'd blame it on archangels,
prophecies broadcast between the leaves
of ordinary trees in the orchard:
*those who restrain desire do so because
theirs is weak enough to be restrained...*
As in Martinsville, Wisconsin, when we
allowed Mike Meinholz to get in the car,
surely a mistake, since the wheels would start
churning up the twelve-packs of Budweiser
he never restrained himself from drinking.
We all have our excuses for wanting
to avoid conversation with mortals,
to restrain ourselves from the fools we are
in the neon light that only darkens
with beer, fears we can never quite drown.
One hundred people trapped in one small town
with just one bar, one church, and one butcher.
Expect poison from standing water,
bewildering Blake would probably say,
if he'd been around to help drag the drunk
from my Impala, down our steep driveway,
to the back lawn where he would sleep, where we
stood that night without the assistance
of good sense, grass, or Romantic verse,
and heard, I swear, a voice come from below
where the woods dropped into the gulley:
a woman in pain, we thought at first,
which nearly made us run the other way,
but then it shrieked like a snared rabbit,
or was it some keening itch branches scratched,
or nothing but a dull thud in the chest,
nothing but what we wanted it to be, then,

some housecat that couldn't find its way down,
some worried awe that barely held us up,
some trembling thing in a tree we couldn't see.

GEORGE BILGERE

Muscle

One minute
I'm standing in the parking lot
behind the De Anza theater. We're throwing our empties

at each other, our smokes turning a whiter
shade of pale.
The subject is horsepower,

and the cars we're leaning on
are Cougars,
Mustangs, GTOs.

Now and then we rumble off
and back again
for no particular reason.

Just to hear the anger, *basso profundo,*
from a 389 V8, as rendered
by a righteous pair of Hooker headers.

When suddenly,
through a dirty, underhanded
trick of time, I'm turning gray

at a table in front of Starbucks.
Sipping a latte, talking mortgage
with a woman I seem to be married to.

A silly little Prius
scoots by without a sound,
followed by a bleak Insight.

MICHELLE BOISSEAU

Eighteenth-Century Boisseau House

Virginia, after a WPA photo

Leafless tree shadow scribbles its face
and shadows of deflated bushes flood
the yard, an arrogant silver squalor
so riddled and clumped it seems a crowd
had barged about, then despaired of raising
a response from such a blank and pointless house.

Bare weatherboard of equivocal
color, snaggle-toothed shutters.
The place couldn't look better
for how bad it looks. Mythic,
Faulknerian. With a satisfying smack
of the cartoon. A place you'd discover

a goat enjoying the taste of mantle.
Shirts tugged from an off-stage clothesline
and flung beside the sway-back steps
turn out to be chickens, a couple
strutting roosters, and a lone peahen.
Someone has been working here,

patching the roof? carrying it off?
A long glaring ladder meets, tweezers-like,
its crisp leaning shadow—the two long legs
of a huge bodiless being who's about to stride
over the fields and trees, over the excellent
fires made when old wood starts to burn.

Monstrance

I don't believe in ghosts though I've seen
milk-steam wandering a darkened room.

I don't believe a big mind regards
all sparrows though I admire the faithful,

how crossing a street or a continent
of trouble they seem confident and frank

as stars. Cranky and cratered, I maneuver
like a moon of bright remarks.

In famous churches when the chanting
carries me into the showy moment—

hoc est enim corpus meum—the golden
rays lifted, bells shaken, incense tempest,

and I'm moved by what I don't believe,
I don't envy believers any more

than I envy beauty its ease, the ocean
its industry. The sun its long and lonely life.

BRUCE BOND

Ringtone

As they loaded the dead onto the gurneys
to wheel them from the university halls,
who could have predicted the startled chirping
in those pockets, the invisible bells
and tiny metal music of the phones,
in each the cheer of a voiceless song.
Pop mostly, Timberlake, Shakira, tunes
never more various now, more young,
shibboleths of what a student hears,
what chimes in the doorway to the parent
on the line. Who could have answered there
in proxy for the dead, received the panic
with grace, however artless, a live bird
gone still at the meeting of the strangers.

ELIZABETH BRADFIELD

Phrenology

Were the earth a skull, the lump
at its base would read to Victorian
doctors as *amativeness:* connubial
love, procreative lust. And where the peninsula

stretches up toward Patagonia
a smidge of *philoprogenitiveness,*
parental love, a fondness for pets
and the generally helpless. Jules Dumont d'Urville,

man of his times, had his own skull mapped
before sailing to map earth's southern blur.
Were the earth a skull and someone
with knowledge laid hands on it, felt topography

for expression of its psyche, would this
answer what questions are asked
in slog and observation, in sample and ice core?

Sub-Antarctic islands bulge at the spot
of *combativeness:* self-defense, a go-to
disposition and love of debate. *Aimentiveness*
at South Africa and New Zealand: appetite,

an enjoyment of food and drink. Jules
was pleased with what the doctor found,
felt himself seen truly. But what judges
our human descriptions of place?

Weather? Lichens? The transitory animals
that touch upon it? Were the earth a skull,
were its bones shaped by humors,
were understanding so palpable, so constant.

JAMES BROWN

Missing the Dead

She's already fallen twice, first breaking the left hip when she misses a step at the beauty parlor, then her right in a tumble at her old house in Arizona. It's in this precarious condition that my mother comes back into my life. When her second husband dies, it falls on me, as her only surviving child, to move her from Arizona to the Shandin Hills Retirement Community in San Bernardino, where I can better attend to her various needs. She is eighty-two. I am forty-seven in this story. My mother and I have never been close; for nearly twenty years we rarely even spoke, and now, for the first time in my adult life, I am forging something of a relationship with her.

Both hips have been replaced, but it's the left one that troubles her. In the short while that she's been here, hardly a couple of months, I've taken her to the doctor three times, and I am taking her there again, today, for another cortisone shot. Hopefully it will relieve some of the pain and stiffness. When I come to pick her up, she is already waiting for me at the front door of her apartment. She has on one of her favorite dresses, a black and white ensemble, and her face is made up with lipstick and the heavy rouge that many older women like to wear. Clearly she's been preparing for hours, as she might for a date if she were younger, and it makes me think: How this mundane experience of visiting a doctor is by no means mundane to someone whose health is faltering, who lives alone and seldom gets out. I should also mention that she is wearing heels, heels I believe may one day be the death of her.

"Mom," I say, "I wish you'd wear flats."

"I like my heels," she says. "I've worn heels all my life."

It's about pride. I understand this. It's about refusing to accept the rapidly narrowing boundaries of her life, and I respect this as well, but with two artificial hips she doesn't so much walk as teeter. I trail closely behind her as we make our way along the path to the carports, ready to catch her if she stumbles, afraid that each step might be her last.

I recently traded in my old BMW for a truck, and because it rides higher than most cars, it is difficult for my mother to pull herself up and into the passenger seat. To make her life easier, I built a strong wooden box for her to use as a step, and while I'm getting this box out from the bed of the truck, after I set it on the ground and unlock the door, I turn around and she is gone. I look down the path we just walked. She's not there. I look in the opposite direction. Nothing, no one. Then, out of sheer luck, I spot her just as she's turning the corner at the end of the carports.

"Mom," I call out.

She doesn't hear me.

"Mom," I call out again, louder, as I begin to run.

She's gone from sight now, heading where I have absolutely no idea, but I catch up with her a few seconds later. I'm out of breath. I touch her arm to get her attention. She turns and looks at me. She studies my face, and for a moment she doesn't quite recognize me. Slowly, though, it dawns on her.

"Where'd you go?" she says.

"I didn't go anywhere."

"Don't leave me like that," she says.

I put my arm around her and smile. "I didn't leave you. I'm right here. C'mon," I say, "the truck's back this way."

*

The pain-relieving effects of cortisone are short lived. The shots also don't always work, and apparently that's the case with my mother. The pain persists. The stiffness gets worse. Walking even a short distance winds her, and in the few weeks since her last doctor's visit she's developed a limp.

Certainly I want her to get better.

Certainly I don't want her to live in pain, and it wouldn't be so bad, having to shuttle her back and forth to the doctor, having to do her grocery shopping and banking, if I didn't sometimes feel that by helping her I'm betraying the memory of my family.

For the longest time, as a child, I denounced her for forging my father's name on the deed of trust to our house and selling it out from underneath us to cover her bad debts. For the longest time, as a child, I denounced her for constantly belittling my brother and sister, for nothing they did ever being good enough, for striking them too hard, too often. For the longest time, as a child, I denounced her for burning down an apartment building, an act that led to her incarceration; and when she was released two years later, I denounced her for taking us children from our father and moving to L.A. But most of all I came to blame her for the suicide of my alcoholic brother, a blame that lasted far beyond childhood, and one that may well have continued if I hadn't eventually come to better understand my own alcoholism. The root causes of addiction share linkage with the past, but in the end no one but the alcoholic is responsible for his destruction. This I learn through experience.

We are in my truck now, headed for my mother's two o'clock doctor appointment, a follow-up for the ineffective cortisone shot. As we drive, I glance over at her, and it strikes me, how as death nears the aged diminish, the body drawing into itself, the limbs thinning to little more than skin and bone. Time has rendered her once quick, violent hands powerless.

"I just want to thank you," she says.

"For what?"

"For taking me around all the time. I don't know what I'd do without you."

I appreciate her words. It is this arrangement, with me caring for her, or else a convalescent home, and she's not ready for that. I'm not ready to ask it of her, either, though I know the day may come when her life drains too much from my own, when she can no longer do even the smallest things for herself. Frail and weak, her beauty long faded, she is harmless now, this woman who my brother, sister and I feared, loved, and hated. As she stares straight ahead, her delicate fingers laced together and folded neatly in her lap, I glimpse the child in my mother, looking impossibly young, looking impossibly old.

*

This time the doctor recommends X-rays, speculating that maybe the steel rod in my mother's left thigh has somehow come loose. If so, it could be the cause of her suffering, and in the meantime, until he has these X-rays, he writes her a prescription for *Feldene*, a mild analgesic similar to aspirin. A few days later, I drive my mother to the Palm Imaging Institute on 21st Street, directly across from Saint Bernardine's Medical Center, where my ex-wife, Heidi, died soon after giving birth to another man's child. Being near this place sets off a wave of hard memories, and I suddenly feel the thirst for a drink, a tightening in the back of my throat. I get out of the truck. I go around to my mother's side and help her do the same. She's heard me talk about this hospital.

"That's where she died, isn't it?"

"Yes."

"Your brother," she says. "Your sister. Your dad and now Heidi. You've lost too many. We've both lost too many."

In the radiology room, my mother lies on a stainless steel table. It is dark in here, just a dim light in one corner, and the machinery is large and old, painted gunmetal gray. The X-ray device slides along two heavy iron rods bolted to the ceiling above her, and as she rests there, her left hip positioned toward the lens, I think about her words. I think about how I can't go there, to the past and the places it takes me, because it takes me too far, and I need to remember the present. I need to remember I have three sons who need me here, who need me now. I need to remember that my second wife has come forward with her own love for my children and that this love is strong and genuine, and that they are fortunate to have her, as I am. I need also to realize that I can't fully love and appreciate this woman, the way she deserves to be loved and appreciated, if I'm constantly obsessed with the past. I am wasting her life by residing in another. It's about balance. It's about loving the living and missing the dead and I have never been able to clearly separate the two.

The radiologist motions for me to step behind the safety partition. Through a pane of thick glass, I watch my mother, wondering why she and I are still here and the others are not, if it's about fate or chance, if it's purposeless or somehow by design. The radiologist presses a switch and a collision of atoms blast through my mother's body, bone, flesh, and skin.

*

My mother is returning from an afternoon bingo game at the recreation center when she takes a spill into a flower bed. This happens between doctor visits, before we get the results of her recent X-rays, and I don't know if the fall has anything to do with her wearing heels or not. Fortunately, though, the soil is moist and soft and serves to break her fall. A passerby helps her to her feet and escorts her back to the apartment, where she phones me just as I'm sitting down to dinner with my wife and sons.

"Jimmy," she says, "I need you to drive me to the hospital."

"What happened?"

She tells me, and I shake my head.

"Did you break anything?"

"I hope not," she says. "But you should see my arm, it's completely black-and-blue."

"Can you move it?"

"It hurts when I do."

"But you can move it. That's a good sign," I say. "Hang on, I'm on my way."

The closest hospital is Saint Bernardine's, but I have no confidence in their doctors or staff. So I take my mother to a much better hospital in the neighboring city of Loma Linda, and on the way there she thanks me again. For driving her to the hospital. For in general looking after her. "I don't know what I'd do without you," she says, as she often does, and that thought apparently triggers another, one about my brother and sister. "It'd be so much easier if Barry and Marilyn were alive. I'm sorry," she says, "that you have to do all this alone." I tell her it's not a problem. I tell her I want to help, and for a while she's quiet. For a while she just sits there holding her injured arm. "I don't know why they did it," she says. "Barry was doing so good as an actor. It's what he always wanted and he went so far, so quickly. I don't understand. And Marilyn, poor Marilyn, she was such a sweet girl. I don't know what got into her."

At one time, her words would've set me off. At one time, I would've told her that she was in many ways responsible for their suicides. I would've wanted her to admit guilt. I would've wanted her to acknowledge the lack of guidance she provided. I would've wanted to acknowledge my part in it all as well, if there was anything I could've done to save them and did not. But as the years have passed, and continue to pass, I have come to realize the worthlessness of guilt and blame and how hurt only begets more hurt.

"You holding up all right?" I ask.

"It aches bad."

"We're almost there," I say. "I'm sure they'll give you some pain medication."

At the Emergency Room, we're assigned a number and asked to wait. It proves a long wait, too, because the place is packed with the sick and injured, mostly the poor and undocumented. Finally, six hours later, we're called in. By this time the bruise has spread from just above her wrist to just below her shoulder, and its darkened in color, a deep purple. I worry that she may have seriously hurt herself. I worry that her bones may have shattered. But when the results of her X-rays come back, the doctor tells us that it's only a hairline fracture to the upper portion of her arm. It will heal on its own. The severe bruising, he says, is common, particularly to the elderly. Oddly this good news seems to disappoint my mother, hungry for attention, any attention, and as we're leaving she whispers in my ear.

"He can't be right," she says. "We need to get another opinion."

But I don't want to think about any more doctors or X-rays, at least not now, not for a while, because I'm tired. I'm worn out. I drop my mother off at her apartment. I help her inside, and on the drive home, along a narrow highway that winds up into the San Bernardino Mountains, an old memory resurfaces: We are in our bedroom, my brother Barry and I, he is twelve and I am six, and she is beating him about the back with a bamboo spear we bought at Disneyland. The tip is made of rubber, but the bamboo is real enough, and she strikes him repeatedly, until he's cowering in the corner. All I do is watch. As the youngest I escape the beatings my sister and brother endure, but later when she leaves, when Barry takes off his shirt, I will remember the many welts and the crisscross patterns they make across his back, already darkening, a deep purple, like the colors of the bruise spreading along my mother's arm.

*

The X-rays are in. These are the ones of her left hip, and once again I am driving my mother to the doctor's office. I am hoping the X-rays will reveal nothing out of the ordinary. I am hoping this appointment is not the precursor to an operation and that the doctor has discovered another, less serious cause for her pain. Going under the knife at her age can easily lead to infection, and infection for the elderly is often a death sentence. Ideally what ails her is something that can be managed with a pill, or physical therapy, and luckily this appears to be the case.

"Your X-rays look fine," the doctor says. "No breaks to the hip. The rod is aligned. I think you may have arthritis, which is not so bad. We can treat that. I'll write you a prescription for the pain and stiffness and I'd like to see you back here in a couple of weeks. Now," he says, "let's take a look at that arm."

Again, just as it happened in the ER, my mother seems oddly dissatisfied with the doctor's diagnosis. I am guessing here but I imagine that she'd anticipated the worst, and instead of being relieved by the better news, she somehow feels jilted. How can the cause *not* be more serious? She doesn't see herself as a complainer, and neither do I, but I'm glad she won't have to risk another operation. The visit ends with the doctor recommending yet another set of X-rays, these for the injured arm, just to be sure it's healing correctly.

Back at her apartment, I fix us both a vodka tonic.

After six months of abstinence, I am drinking again. I have been drinking off and on for the last several weeks, and trying, as I have often done in the past and failed, to limit myself to just a few, and only when the day is over, only when my work is done. I make mine strong, nearly straight up, and I make my mother's weak, so she won't get woozy when she stands up after I've left. She relaxes in the leather La-Z-Boy that I bought her, and I sit across from her on the couch.

Of course, she knows about my problem, but she has no say over what I do, and, besides, she likes a drink now and then herself. It loosens the tongue. It allows us to talk freely where we might ordinarily freeze up. Still, as I hand her her drink, she feels inclined to at least warn me.

"Be careful," she says. "Remember what happened to your sister and brother. I couldn't bear to lose my last child."

"Don't worry," I tell her. "I'm fine. I have it under control."

On the coffee table I notice a framed snapshot of my mother and her husband, not my father but her second husband, posing on the sands in Hawaii, his arm draped across her shoulders, both wearing leis and smiling into the camera. She sees me staring at it.

"He was a good man," she says. "Not to slight your father, but Bud always did those little things. Flowers or perfume when I wasn't expecting it. You know we went to Hawaii not once but three times. I can't say your Dad ever took me on a real vacation."

She fails to mention that she bankrupted my father. She fails to mention that she bankrupted her second husband not once but three times in the twenty-five years they were married and that these trips to Hawaii were made before and between those bankruptcies.

"That's nice," I say, and for the most part I mean it.

Because they look happy in the picture. And it would be wrong of me, I think, to begrudge anyone what little happiness they take from this life, whether I believe they deserve it or not.

"He went so fast. He just kissed me goodnight and we fell asleep and when I woke up he was cold. His skin was blue." She takes a sip of her drink and sets it back down. "It's hard," she says, "living alone after all those years. I appreciate your staying and visiting for a while. I know you're busy. I know you have a family." She pauses. "It's strange, awful even, how quickly it goes. I hope there's an afterlife, but I really don't believe in it."

I fix us another drink. I stay for a while longer and then I tell her I need to leave, that my wife is teaching a night class and it's my turn to make dinner for the boys. At my house, I head upstairs to the bedroom to change into some sweatpants and a T-shirt, and as I'm doing this I look at another picture, one on my dresser, a framed black-and-white photograph of my mother and father taken shortly after they married. I pick it up. I hold it toward the light. In this picture, my mother is thirty. My father, beginning to bald, is forty-four. They make a handsome pair with his sharp jaw line, blue-gray eyes and fair skin, and my mother's olive complexion, her dark Sicilian eyes and thick black hair. In her day she was a striking woman, and I wonder if this has anything to do with it, her beauty, if it somehow predisposed her to expect more from life than life was willing to give.

I don't know.

I don't know a lot of things about my mother. I don't know a lot of things about my father, either, or of the other photos I find after his funeral, in the bottom of a box, faded snapshots of Barry and Marilyn and myself, just a baby, when for a short while we resembled something of a family.

*

At this point, I lose count of the X-rays and doctor appointments. I resign myself once again to another visit to the Palm Imaging Institute for the hairline fracture to her arm and then, of course, the follow-up with the doctor to make sure that arm is healing correctly. They've become a nuisance, these trips, and I'm losing more time now than I'm willing to forsake. But I also realize that she's my duty, my care and responsibility.

At the age of fourteen I leave her, my brother, and sister in Los Angeles and return to my father in San Jose, nearly four hundred miles across the state. I don't know how it is that my mother and I first give up on each other, who doesn't return the others calls, or letters, if it's me, the irresponsible teenager, or her, the negligent parent. Who misses whose birthday? Who forgets to send a Christmas card, let alone a present? Although this sort of carelessness contributes to our estrangement, it is Barry's suicide that drives us furthest apart, accounting for our nearly twenty years of relative silence. And ironically it is suicide again, this time my sister's, that brings us back together. We are the sole survivors of a family that seems almost fated to self-destruct, like a deadly affliction, or even a curse, and time for us is running out.

I pick her up a full hour early.

The Palm Imaging Institute isn't more than a few miles away, and I've arrived in plenty of time, but my mother feels otherwise.

"What took you so long?" she says. "Now we have to rush."

I don't argue. I don't see the point. In my truck, she informs me that we also need to do her grocery shopping after the X-rays, that she needs stamps, too, which means a trip to the post office, and since the bank is right next door she'd like to drop in there as well. Her dry cleaning, she says, can wait until next week, though she brings it with her in a brown paper bag "just in case it's not too much trouble to swing by the cleaners on the way back."

I take a deep breath.

The day will be longer than I expected, and here is how I see it unfolding: There will be more X-rays, if not for this injury, then another. There will be more doctor visits, too, more prescriptions to fill, and I don't suppose, no matter what I tell myself, or how hard I might try, that my mother and I will ever be very close. As a parent myself I can imagine nothing more devastating than losing a child to suicide, and for my mother there can be no abdication, no resolution, no peace. This is something we will both take to the grave, as my father does for his oldest son, never understanding, never reconciling, and it is good that he at least dies before his daughter. I don't suppose I'll ever entirely forgive my mother, just as I am certain there are those who will never entirely forgive me. In this way, we are the same, and when our days together have fallen to the past, when only the memories remain, I hope to discover the difference between loving the living and missing the dead.

ROBERT CORDING

Gift

> *How long can one man's lifetime last?*
> —Wang Wei

Long enough, he said to our tears,
to know *all of it is a gift*. We wanted
to hold him back from the dying

he was busy doing, nine months of working
his way through the Book of Subtractions:
first the relished taste of food and wine,

and then Yeats, the *Four Quartets,*
and the Psalms he could no longer read
alone. In the end, even the music

his children loaded on an iPod—
Mozart and Brahms to counter the morphine
that countered the bladed pains

that ran through his back—
became too difficult to listen to.
And yet he called each painful day a gift,

and held fiercely to each moment,
whatever it brought: swallows freelancing
in the wind, the odor of lilac

after a night's rain, the way sunlight settled
over the rug like a large dog—
nothing he earned, but accepted,

as he accepted the near identical looks
his children and his wife exchanged
when they saw how, daily, his cancer grew

towards the dread of his utter absence.
To all of it he said *yes*.
Yes to the pollen greening the roofs

of parked cars as his body withered,
and to the cold of the window glass
he leaned his cheek against,

and *yes*, to the nearly unendurable love
he felt for his wife and children
whose longing for him he could not

lessen, and to everything that remained
unsayable between them. And *yes*,
finally, to whatever came next, after

this life he had been given, this death.

CHAD DAVIDSON

Labor Days

I woke to a blizzard of franchising, burned quickly
the money earned in a dress outlet in a strip mall.
Mornings, I lugged the vacuum into the Versailles

of the communal changing room. From my own image,
a hundred versions regressed in the netherworld
of underwear and slip, which is not so much

confession as compression, years I worked
like a layered look simply keeping me warm.
Life's like that, claimed the register in ten dollar intervals.

It was California, after all, where snow fell
only on TV in fine electricity after baseball, or in the lull
of a Thanksgiving *Twilight Zone* marathon I watched,

stunned by my first taste of store-bought vacation.
How eerily the hours crept along, imperceptible
as the changing fashion of necklines, drawing deeper

into twilight's cleavage. It was the one about the librarian,
Burgess Meredith, who lusted after library stacks,
desired time enough to undress each book.

When his glasses shattered, it wasn't pity I felt,
or justice for how callously he wished away
the kind receptionist. Rather it was pleasure,

or guilt dressed as such, to see him cry blind
to sunlight made text. It's been years
since I wrapped the vacuum's noose

around its neck and stowed it for the last time
in the history of Western civilization.
Though in Rome, in the forum, a tour guide pointed

to a temple's hem and the mildewed sewer underneath.
Etruscan, he said, perhaps much more beyond the white
marble the Caesars robed their city in. A city's no place

to disinter. Rome could hardly carve a subway
tunnel without discovering itself. All around,
the sunken attempts at modernity, a few pillars

stripped and block-cut at the feet of Constantine.
Before the death of cities comes again the glory
of their past. Because atop the Palatine,

the loose leaves of a pizza joint's flyers
scurried about me, and a woman stooped to take one
from the marble's face. How many like her,

in loose summer cotton, have touched there?
How many ways back still exist, as if
we could choose from a menu the very meat

of our becoming? I must have seemed strange
searching the bleached blossoms of her dress,
peeling back the petals, each one revealing more

than its craze of stitch and fiber, which is how life is,
which is how I touched—near the Loggia Mattei,
on the Palatine in Rome, two millennia after

the first stones were laid, past the leafless trees,
over oceans of traffic and sinking monuments—
a shop in southern California, and the first snow of my life.

STEPHEN DUNN

Aesthete

A fire has started in the kitchen,
and is moving from room to room.
There's just enough time
to save the Rembrandt, an original,
or the portrait of your wife.
You save the Rembrandt, of course,
but when you get outside
you think it might be possible
to save the portrait as well.
You dash back in, and rescue
the portrait just before the flames
would have it as their own.
You're half way out the door now,
you're going to be fine
when you realize, oh no, your wife
has been up in the attic sorting through
memorabilia of your lifetime together.
How stupid of me, you say to yourself,
the Rembrandt or my actual wife—
that's what I needed to decide between.
How did I get it so wrong?

To a Friend Accused of a Crime He May Have Committed

We'll never know for sure now,
you in your garage with the motor on
and the tailpipe clogged and the door closed,
three days before the trial. Your wife
found you after she found the note,
and this morning the numinous beauty
of low fog in our field has taken on
a strange gloom, a lone deer grazing there
with an alertness that you must have had
many days of your life, lest you be caught.

For twenty-five years we knew you
to be a man who could charm a room,
yet stand up at a faculty meeting
and press an argument, not back down.
When we dined with you, you loved
to tell us all the places you'd been.
How stupid of you to allow
your computer to be repaired,
the hard facts on the hard drive—
all those boys, girls, this other life.

What brilliance, though, to have concealed it
for so long. And how nearby desperation
always must have been. I'll remember your face
now as a thing with a veil, what I so admire
in poker players. You were not one of those.
When word first got out, we called you,
said we were there for you. In our minds
you remained a friend. We didn't call again.

When does a friend cease being a friend?
After which betrayal, yours or ours?
Or do we just go on in the muck and the mud
holding ourselves up the best we can?
That's what we're asking ourselves,
the fog lifting a little, the newspaper
with your photo in it open on our table.

PETER EVERWINE

Rain

Toward evening, as the light failed
and the pear tree at my window darkened,
I put down my book and stood at the open door,
the first raindrops gusting in the eaves,
a smell of wet clay in the wind.
Sixty years ago, lying beside my father,
half asleep, on a bed of pine boughs as rain
drummed against our tent, I heard
for the first time a loon's sudden wail
drifting across that remote lake—
a loneliness like no other,
though what I heard as inconsolable
may have been only the sound of something
untamed and nameless
singing itself to the wilderness around it
and to us until we slept. And thinking of my father
and of good companions gone
into oblivion, I heard the steady sound of rain
and the soft lapping of water, and did not know
whether it was grief or joy or something other
that surged against my heart
and held me listening there so long and late.

GARY FINCKE

The Art of Moulage

For dermatology, for the betterment
Of medical science, Joseph Towne produced
Over five hundred models of skin disease,
Forming those faces from beeswax and resin,
Applying disease with spatulas and knives—
Lesions and rashes, pustules, and the chancres
Of unchecked syphilis, especially those
On faces disfigured by heredity,
Bad luck, or unwisely satiated lust,

An art, getting sickness just right, and there were
Others, like Jules Baretta, who created
Two thousand moulages, some of which followed
The changes in flesh from first symptom to death.
What's necessary to warn us? Tumors? Wounds?
Neither of those masters would share the secrets
Of his work, refusing to teach the darkness
Of gangrene, the inflammation where it spreads.

My father, near ninety, declares his creased face
Unrecognizable. My friend's mother, whose
Beautiful face was shredded through a windshield,
Lifts her right hand to the dense thicket of scars
When someone approaches... Look, an hour ago,
The harelips splitting the faces of children
Made me turn a page of a news magazine,
Sending me back to the soft community
Of the unscarred that turns away, revolted,
From the terrible commonplace of acne
And shingles; from warts, boils, melanoma—
And yet, with models, we are fascinated
By the possibilities of the body,

What we are capable of turning into,
Misery thriving until our skin becomes
A sieve for horror that rises through the pores.

GREGORY FRASER

Silverfish

Pressed between print, haunting gutters, we traded closeness
for dialogue and plot, dropped concordantly to sleep

not long before dawn, hardbacks propped on our chests
like tents on a plain in Cooper. Wingless, piscatorial,

we dined on starches and molds, slid into cracks, crevices,
bathtubs on occasion. Troubled to escape their slick,

enameled palisades, we chose the horizontal: *Leaves of Grass*
in lounge chairs by the pool, Ginsberg on blow-up rafts.

Our rooms, bibliographic amphitheaters, thronged
with titled spines. *The Odyssey, The Frogs, Collected Verse*

of John Crowe Ransom. We burrowed in Woolf,
gnawed Updike and Austen, all of whom declared,

The first sorrow can be lifted but not hauled off—
a theme we paid too little notice, paying ransom to it,

as we were, for and with our lives. During famine,
we attacked the leatherware: fine-bound collector's copies.

Naturally, we considered children nymphs, creatures
of liquid and myth. A decade's passed since last

we kissed. Were we mistaken to embrace,
or simply overtaken by aversions to the real?

One time, in a viscid afternoon no one but us recalls,
I climbed the broken back of a sweet-gum tree

while you snapped photos, unmindful of your thumb
obscuring the lens. One can block a part of the heart,

you know. You know, *Lepisma saccharina*,
sweet tooth, old friend of sizing and glue. Thankfully,

the damage we did, commensurate with our kind,
was slight—minor foxing of silks and rayon.

Yet I sometimes think we might have flourished
had we canoed the Susquehanna, or submitted

to the balms of church. Studious, antennae raised,
we sought protection in exacted meaning, forced

our minds to mind and called the act *reflection*.
It didn't help. Lost in leitmotifs, humidities

of simmering conflict, we came to begrudge
the characters we consumed—their crafted shapeliness,

perfect aim at fate. Who could blame us in our supple
exoskeletons, lank appendages? We had to part.

Like every paradise, ideal companionship exists purely
on the page, is the page. Here. For old times. Feed on this.

CAROL FROST

Apiary XV

To live without memory is to have each hour
as a pane of air for canvas and the view from a window
to paint: amber-honey cold mornings:
humbled by evening:: variation and variation
of ambiguous figments—ziggurat beehive
auroras—flicker and go out. All history
may as well be in these brushstrokes:
the hand has not rested nor the paint dried.
Before they pull curtains to the sill
Mother show us if you know what radiance
remains: river: your river beneath glacial stone.

Two Songs for Dementia

(Tyrannus tyrannus)
That bird towering: late summer
garden: who senses the burring wings
deep inside roses and like the angel
before all nectar's sipped
before gold scatters in bright air
descends from its high height
to lift away the bee...
not a honey eater: though looking so:
bee after bee disappearing
into incandescence::
Only the metaphysic flower
feels the approach: and emptying.

(Ursinus)
Gold helm scent of honey and the drowsing bear:
golden: begotten of honey: bee larvae
chokeberry sweet clover carrion::
leaving the den in the undergrowth
for sweet-thaw sun-thaw above:
shut out from all the world within:
The valleys and hills feel its feet:
shambling when the sun is low:
slow mouth: Didn't Mother say she felt
its presence a long time?
thought small as atoms,
and aromatic as honey ales:
body manacled—body preserving
small sweetnesses?
until the bear groaned and stretched:
entered there and deeply ate?

Honeymoon

They glowed, the first day after their wedding, like planets in the morning sky, and their movements, no matter the task—packing gifts, choosing deli sandwiches, examining the map—were stately and serene.

The second day, in the car, she said she was homesick. For their wedding, of all things. "It went too fast." He lifted a hand from the steering wheel and playfully traced a heart on her thigh with his fingertip. "This time two days ago," he said, "what were we doing?"

"Getting dressed. Practicing our vows. But now it's over, and everyone's gone home."

The third day, they stood on the deck of a restored clipper ship. The water of the bay was bright and the small waves energetic, but, in her mind, a gale had risen. Beneath her, the clipper ship surged and rolled in a worsening sea and, overhead in the rigging, men clung to the spars. Gusting winds burst the bellies of the sails and the tatters flew wildly in the seething air. Then, a warm hand around hers. A kiss on her cheek. "This is a quiz," he teased, and indicated the gutters running along the edges of the deck. Did she happen to know what they were called? The wind vanished, and the clipper rode dead quiet at the dock. They had joked about his left brain marrying her right. "Scuppers," she snapped, and her voice was mean. He rolled his map into a tight tube, thwacked his thigh, and marched down the gangplank. She watched him board the next ship on the quay without her.

Of course, they made up over lunch. In their room, they dozed and made love, she clinging to his back and snagging her leg around his waist. That evening, near sunset, they crossed the bay on a steam-powered ferryboat. They strolled, they took pictures, and after a while they leaned on a rail and peered down a hatch into the boat's hot belly. The engineer, in kerchief, mustache, and leather apron, lifted a lever the least fraction of an inch, tapped the glass face of a gauge, then poked the blistering black and red coals in the open firebox. Sweat slicked his face and neck and, for a moment, he worked his upper lip and mustache back and forth, as if relieving an itch. The poor man was probably asked a hundred times a day about the heat in the engine room, but her interest was the firebox. How was it that flames moved the old ferry forward?

Simple. The firebox heated the water in the sealed tank above and, once the water was hot enough to raise the pressure in the tank, steam was released, and it was the steam, also under pressure, that drove the pistons and turned the wheel of the boat. The engineer scrubbed his face and neck with his kerchief.

"Do these things ever blow up?" she said.

The engineer wiped a drop of oil from the woodwork. "Not so much," he said, and then asked where they were from. Before they could answer, he said, "I love this boat. I absolutely love this boat."

The fourth day, they walked narrow stone streets named Alpha, Union, Rose, and Omega. They admired the well-preserved houses—high narrow wooden ones, foursquare federal brick, some topped with widow's walks. Mounting blocks remained in place along curbs, herb gardens thrived behind white wood or black cast-iron fences, and old roses climbed trellises. "Imagine the zoning codes," he whispered. "Imagine the social sets," she whispered back. "Like cells under a microscope," he said, "forming and reforming." Three hundred years, and fishing boats still left and returned to the town docks. Three hundred years, and newly built boats still sailed out of this harbor bound for buyers all over the world. They lunched beneath a faded umbrella on a dock. He ambled the quay before the food came, and she resumed reading a novel she'd begun before the wedding.

That night, as they were falling asleep, her thigh across his loins, his arm firm around her shoulders, she lifted her head. "Did you see my bouquet?" She was drying it as a keepsake.

"I'll look." He turned on the lights, checked the wastebaskets, then searched outside on their deck. "Gone," he said.

"Dumpster," she said.

They dressed from their duffel of dirty clothing.

"Oh, let's take the camera," she said.

"Only if it goes in the album. Me with my ass sticking out of a dumpster."

Actually, she wanted to star in this story. *And then I climbed into the dumpster and dug all around, and there it was—*

"It might be gone," she said.

They walked across wet lawns, through pools of light, past three more inn buildings, until they found the dumpsters. He lifted the lid of the first one, and they leaned back, bracing for stench, but the bad smell was slight—fresh trash, she thought. They stood on tiptoe and looked. No need for diving, digging, or heroics of any kind. The browning roses, tied with their broad ivory ribbon, had been flung in last on top of a landslide of tied-tight green garbage bags. He lifted them out, and she took them in her arms. Back in the room, she laid them in a box of bunched tissue paper.

In the morning, he asked if they'd gone spelunking in dumpsters or if he'd only dreamed it.

Later that day, they left the coast and headed inland. She missed the wharves and the thickets of sailboat masts. She missed the sea rolling onto the land and then receding, yet remaining in place all the while. She missed time being alive in all of its layers at once: the ancient natives and early sailors, the centuries-old clam beds and stone houses, the seaworthy dories, catboats, and fiberglass sailboats with strange silver-gray sails. Was it the beat of the ocean that made time pile up instead of forging ahead?

The next few days they would spend in Vermont, in an old brick house on a brook in a hard-to-find village of white houses, inn, post office, and store. Their stay would be a gift from the owners, friends she'd visited once before, briefly, for coffee and a breather on her way elsewhere. She was eager for the house's gentle proportions, the intimacy of low hand-plastered ceilings, and the petite fireplace in the parlor with a window seat over the brook. In the 1920s, the house had belonged to an Iron-Jawed Angel who, along with women whose names are better remembered, had chained herself to the White House fence, vowing to starve to death, if need be, in order to win suffrage for women. She and the others had been shackled, their jaws pried open, and scalding gruel poured down their throats. Remnants of the crusade hung intact on the walls: framed newspaper accounts of suffragettes voting illegally and a fading wool pennant with hand-appliquéd letters: *Votes for Women*. Bookshelves in the hallway, in the foyer, on the landing, were jammed tight with women's biographies, women's histories, women's politics and philosophy and health. What exquisite pleasure to select one of those volumes and read all day in the window seat, leaning into pillows and listening to the brook.

En route, however, he was determined to make one stop. At a small county airport, somewhere off the highway, three World War II planes were scheduled to be on display. He drove and she navigated, directing him when to leave the highway and where to turn on scantily marked two-lane county roads. Occasional arrows pointed toward the airport, but these seemed to have been tacked up by jokesters. He began leaning toward her and trying to read the map while he drove. She held their place with a fingertip and, when a bicyclist zoomed out from a side road, she cried, "Look out!" A few moments later, when the truck in front of them braked suddenly, she cried out again. "Watch out!" Then she added, "If you want to navigate, I'll drive."

He pulled himself upright behind the steering wheel. "Do you see any planes?"

"Not yet."

"I think I'll just pull over and look at the—"

Her arm shot out, angled over the steering wheel. "There."

At the gate, they were charged twenty dollars. The man who collected their money wore a black nylon flight jacket, embroidered with the red, orange, and yellow insignia of some bomb squadron. "We brought a B17, a B24, and a B32."

"Yes, I see," her husband said.

"Your money," the man said. "It all goes to the planes." As if the aircraft were widows and orphans.

They passed the souvenirs, and she pointed to a rack of black flight jackets as garishly embroidered as the ticket taker's. "Now that," she said, "would have been a deal breaker."

He'd stopped to examine a box of shells, certified to have been shot from one of the machine guns on the very same B24 standing thirty feet away on the tarmac. "What?"

"If you wanted me to wear that. That jacket." Her hand dropped. "Never mind."

She stood near the hangar and watched him circle the tail of the B17. He reached up for the rudder, then retraced his steps and looked up to study the engine and propeller. A man beside him apparently made a remark, and her husband—*husband*—pointed at something and responded. The two men walked toward the aluminum ladder propped against the open hatch, and the other man climbed up, her husband following.

From outside the plane, she saw his head and shoulders in the rounded glass hood of the cockpit. Together the two men seemed to look down at the pilot's instruments, then out toward the horizon. They disappeared, then reappeared, crouch-walking past the open hatch. Again they vanished, and then she saw familiar calves in familiar pale khakis, bare ankles, and scuffed boat shoes tightroping along an interior catwalk. A brilliant light burst from the waist gunner's window. She gasped and jerked back.

"Only a camera, honey." An older woman in tan orthopedic shoes and a pale chiffon scarf moved closer. "But it sure scares you to pieces."

She grew anxious for all of him to break into view.

"Don't even think of going in," the woman said. "First there's that ladder, and then you can't stand up straight in that cockpit. It's not nice, not at all, and there's that part where you'd have to balance." She was pointing to the place that seemed to require the tightroping. "That's the bomb bay, you know. It's greasy. And it certainly wasn't open like that when they flew. My husband—"

Khaki cuffs, bare ankles, and boat shoes appeared on the far side of the plane. A step, another step, and he was visible from the knees down, then the waist down, and then the whole of the man she married was free of one bomber and moving away toward the next.

"Excuse me," she said, and made for the ladder of the B17.

The older woman was right. You crawled on your hands and knees, then did something nearly impossible with your back in order to lift your head and shoulders forward and up into the roped-off cockpit. The barrel of the machine gun pointed into the sky, and a belt of brass shells, larger than she'd imagined and hanging in heavy-bottomed loops, was threaded through the weapon, ready for firing. She duck-walked past the open hatch, then stood up straight in the bomb bay. In front of her was the narrow beam that she must tiptoe along. The tarmac was visible fifteen feet below. Finally, hands out and ready to grab an empty bomb cradle if necessary, she slid one foot forward, and took one, two, three deliberate steps.

Ahead of her, in the waist of the bomber, a man was talking. He wore a tweed suit, but no necktie. Inside a jacket pocket, his hand seemed to rattle dice. "A gunner," he said. "Pop was a gunner." She neared the end of the beam, then stepped onto the seamed and riveted floor of the plane. "He told us a story once." His hand continued working in his pocket. "Only once, and right near the end of his life. It was something he wanted us to know." He looked out through the exit and back at his listener, a man in his sixties, baseball cap with an insignia, and a navy blue golf jacket.

She eased toward the wall of the plane, pretending not to listen. The crew who'd flown this plane to this out-of-the-way-airport had tossed their gear along the bulkhead: black backpacks, a six-pack-sized blue and white cooler, and an army-green first aid kit.

"I forget which mission this was, what number, but they were down close and drawing fire, then really caught it from those flak guns. Pop was the navigator, and didn't get hit. Nobody got hit, but when they got up and out of it, turned out the belly was all torn up."

"He came back, though. Your pop." The other man touched his foot here and there, as if this plane too might have been shot from below.

"They had no landing gear—shot to hell. No wheels, and they'd already delivered their load."

"Crash landing?"

The man in the tweed jacket pointed at the floor behind the bomb bay. Heavy wheels were poised in a shiny, heavily-slotted track. "Know what that is? The hatch down into the ballgunner's turret."

"It moves on the wheels?" she heard herself say.

The men glanced at her.

"The cover does. It closes off the turret." The man made a fist in his pocket. "Which is why suddenly they're hearing the ball gunner screaming, *Kill me! Kill me!* Just begging."

"I don't get it," said the man in the blue jacket.

Oh, she got it all right.

"He was shot," she said quietly. "Along with the landing gear."

"Nope." The storyteller turned toward her. "Not even a nick."

She held very still. But if the gunner hadn't been shot?

"I don't get it," the man in the navy blue jacket said again.

"Don't you see? They have to crash land, and the turret gunner—"

"Your dad survived." The man tugged on the brim of his cap. "Lots of guys died, in those landings."

The navigator's son pointed down at the ball turret hatch. "That poor bastard knew he'd never make it. Dad said the screaming—"

She moved past the men, toward the exit. She'd heard enough.

"So there was a pact."

"Holy Jesus."

"They stood right here. In a circle."

She looked over her shoulder, and the hand of the navigator's son shaped itself into a loose pistol.

"They stood right here and on the count of three—"

Her foot was solid on the wooden steps, then lighter somehow on the tarmac. Turning, she gazed at the ball turret. It hung from the belly of the plane like a huge glass egg. She looked up at the wing over her head, still seeing only the ball turret, rinsed with blood.

Her name was being called. She could hear it, but the dead ball gunner held her a while longer. Bones, sinews, cock, and dreams— shapeless sludge. She looked again at the wing overhead. Not a plane tour for history buffs. A flying mausoleum.

She turned and her husband was there. "I lost you," he said, and she felt, specifically, how his right arm went up and across her back on a diagonal, and his left found its way around her waist. "Where were you?"

He let her make a little room between them, and she glanced over her shoulder at the brown purposeful plane.

"You went in?" he said.

She nodded. "A man in there told a story about a ball gunner. He got trapped. And the rest of them pulled their guns—"

"Sidearms," he said gently.

She nodded again, her head against his shoulder.

"I can't believe you went in. I'm proud of you." He checked her over as if she herself had flown a mission. He tucked a loose lock of hair behind her ear. Immediately, it blew free again. "Come on," he said. "Let's take your picture. You went in! We'll take it right up here. You stand by that propeller."

And so she did, not touching it and not smiling for the first picture or two. He looked at her over the top of the camera and grinned mischievously, as if he'd once again found something new and startling about her. She laughed then, and came back to herself, to whoever she was now. She moved in close, reached up along the propeller, and smiled cockily into the camera lens.

Finally, they were going somewhere.

ALLEN GROSSMAN

The Garden Oak

1.
Once more. My obligation to my mind
requires that I speak in the only way
it understands.—This time, of the oldest tree
remembered, the garden oak in its mysterious well

which utters still, each spring—after winter
and all its snows—new branches, and on them
leaves. Then flowers—and, then its proper seeds,
each acorn in a cup, each also an oak

to be remembered, an oak in just such
a remembered garden as this one is.
Sit down with me. I have more to say...
And there is honor in finding the words.

2.
NOTE! I am not a speaker of your kind.
No one you hear is a speaker of your kind.
The first poet I knew, my only master, was
not human, not a speaker of our kind.

Honor is repeating words good enough—
mute, eloquent, and true—as uttered by the garden
oak, rooted in its mysterious well, when the wind
rose up and the oak uttered words, and taught.

Whatever I may have said to you, or to
another (it's now fifty years of saying),
whatever in or around the words seems
for a moment true, is of no account unless

3.
you hear the oak say it too. Such is the way,
reason of rememembering. Listen! It is not I
who speak. You do not attend to me, alone.
Above us both, above each one, the master

of winters rooted in a mysterious well,
makes words known.—Something knocks at the window.
It is thought of the world without intention,
without naming and without a name, or

the idea of name. Now it is brought to mind—
enormous sway, without love or intention to love.
All my life, I sit in the shadow of the oak,
spectator of its changes—and the weather.

4.
Come out with me and feel the enormous sway
of one will that's free. Although dark and rain
shroud body and soul. Although you are weary
and cold as hell, be patient with my words

and sing along with me. I am like you.
You are like me—on the same road—and each
of us has a story. We are not free.
Nor are we slaves. We are not lost. Not found.

There is a tree we know—the two of us—
the garden oak, rooted in a mysterious well.
Under that tree, master of seasons, sit down
a moment. Consider. Then go your way.

R. S. GWYNN

Body Politic

> *The provinces of his body revolted.*
> —W. H. Auden, "In Memory of W. B. Yeats"

The histories are rife with various versions.
Some of them cite those first covert incursions
Of double agents turned far to the south
And sent north to the land's unwary mouth
(As if it *had* a mouth), smuggling their goods
Into the hearts of common neighborhoods.
Those who received them, ordinary men
Or women (sometimes children) took them in
First as diversions, then necessities.
We have the testimony; some of these
Survived because they overcame their need,
But others, many others, came to feed
Exclusively on that which did them harm,
Ignoring every warning, each alarm.

Soon enough there were signs at the frontiers—
Misrule at the extremities, or ears
(As if a state *had* ears) that sometimes heard
A threat lurking behind an honest word,
An accusations hidden in a prayer,
Or even laughter. Then, in the clear air,
The edgy guards discharged their guns on throngs
and singing songs
Yet were perceived as dangers. Nonetheless,
The priests and prophets who arrived to bless
The fallen found their wounds were not severe
But, left untreated, brought within a year
Not death but *fear* of it, which is the curse
That, growing, made the situation worse.

Shortages ensued; the nation's diet
(It *had* to eat) faltered. Uneasy quiet
Descended. Outages conspired to stall
The progress of the citizenry, all
Who saw their own decline (for they *had* sight)
Vaguely in blackouts, clearly when the light
Of morning in their mirrors showed them faces
That held no subtle hints, no former traces
Of honor, say, or beauty in the thin
And unfamiliar slackening of the skin,
The loosening of teeth (yes, *these* as well).
In glass constricted like a prison cell
They learned at last that damage had been done
And pulled their shades against the lucent sun.

The chronicles agree, page laid on page,
The times then dying were their golden age.
The end was hard: the capital surrounded
By God knows who can say, the pits and mounded
Earthworks braced with furniture and manned
By small, unruly children, the unplanned
And futile exodus through sewers and drains
Of those who missed the final desperate planes.
The Head of State (it *had* a head) declared
Resistance would continue, but few shared
His faith, such as it was, they could go on
And dropped their weapons, every stick and stone.
Confusion reigned, communications died,
And all went over to the Victor's side.

"It came. We saw it," patriots declared
While others shrugged their shoulders, blindly stared,
And spat into the gutters. Monuments
To lost ideals were hauled for scrap but since
There was no industry were hauled away
And sunk for jetties to prolong the bay.
Some species thrived while others disappeared,
And with each day a deepening evening neared.
No poet in the nation had the heart

(The *public* heart) to trust the powers of art
To mend its soul (it had *this* too). Thus, joy
Perished with a lost child's unbroken toy
A soldier plucked from the shell-crusted mud
And tossed away into the ebb and flood.

RACHEL HADAS

Leaning In

Students all too commonly misconstrue the
poem in which Sappho calls that man equal
to a god, who, opposite you, leans in and
    whispers, etcetera,

tending to assume it's about two people:
speaker/loved one? Beloved and man near her,
bending close to her, whom the poet hears as,
    heads close together,

they laugh softly? Wait: that makes three. Sweat's pouring
down some body: his? hers? whose? At which point I
throw my hands up, figurative or literal,
    and the chalk shatters.

I'd...been going to diagram the poem:
speaker; loved one; man sitting near the loved one—
the luck of him! The nerve of him! Almost equal,
    if one dare say this

(Phrase Catullus added in his rendition:
"*si fas es*"): he almost surpasses gods, who
sits across from you, who drinks in, etcetera.
    So: a triangle

that I could have sketched on the blackboard. Never
mind. Hands, bodies seeking each other? Cell phones,
Blackberries, incessant barrage of message...
    And that beloved:

now my glossary has been infiltrated
by the use of "loved one" in life's new context
to denote the man who has oh so slowly
   turned to a problem

soluble finally by what some call "placement"
(one Canadian doctor said "disposition").
Love? Let lyrics rich with their clustering pronouns
   do the embracing.

But there is no doubt that I'm now familiar
with the template. Three in a room: first doctor;
husband next; and finally me, caregiver,
   leaning in, listening.

Tu Ne Quaesieris

after Horace Odes I.11

However candid, wise, courageous,
and charming the neurologist, it was
surely a mistake for her to say
that thirty years might stretch ahead of me
living with who I lived with. And yet I
had asked her, silly as Leuconoe.
Scire nefas! Besides, how could she tell
quem mihi finem di dederint? All
who wish such knowledge, listen up: just let
life happen. When my sister called the vet
for Lefty's last appointment, it was she,
not Jupiter, who issued the decree
(not *plures hiemes* but one last hour),
moved not at all by any lust for power
but by the simple, stark necessity
of ending a beloved's misery.
Debarred from putting anyone to sleep,
I pick up Horace, watch the poem leap
and flare into today's cold urgency,
living within which, *spatio brevi,*
I prune back hope, pour wine, and raise my glass:
Sufficient unto. "Carpe diem." Don't ask.

MARY STEWART HAMMOND

Facing Eternity

Automobiles rout the Eternal City,
their exhaust peeling like slow acid
the skin and cartilage off statues,
slipping the spirit from its moorings, as
a million times a day, humans stand,
backs pressed to the wall in the narrow streets,
to let cars pass. One step, two, sometimes
maybe even a string of uninterrupted steps, then,
backs to the wall, they bide their time,
while two, three, four, even a string of cars
and motor bikes growl and whine and buzz and honk,
threading through parked cars and pedestrians.
Even automobiles are brought to a standstill
by automobiles—eighteen, twenty, abandoned
in random clots that barricade the streets.
Only humans able to climb like monkeys
from fender to hood to fender can pass,
rage rising like the heat off baked metal,
like the woman in Ferragamo heels and Armani
using feet and hands and bum to clamber
over one such tangle, fuming in Italian, "In no
other country in the world...!" But mostly,
humans stand quietly, our backs to the wall,
our backs to the wall, our backs to the wall,
acting out the place we've come to.

Portrait of My Husband Reading Henry James

    Rather, it is in the shorter history of America,
not England, not Italy, that we find ourselves
in the perfect middle of a rainy summer afternoon
inside a 1930s shingled boathouse long since
beached on a low hill out of water's reach,
and plumbed and electrified for habitation.
No effort has been made to hide its origins.
Old masts and spars wait in the overhead rafters.
Blocks and tackle, coiled in figure eight knots,
loop from hooks on the wooden walls' open studs.
The faded blue transom of Will o' the Wisp,
my mother-in-law's 1920s childhood Sneakbox,
hangs on its traveler over the west window as if
the bow and midship had sailed into the dark wood.

    The person concerned sprawls in a Bean shirt
and Top-Siders in an easy chair by a slow fire
crackling like balled up paper uncrumpling,
the length of him spilling on and on out over the ottoman.
He is meeting Isabel Archer, Madame Merle,
and Gilbert Osmond while Duke Ellington's smooth
rationalizations slide out of speakers in a tease
of intrigues and blue notes played behind the beat,
major chords changing to minor, piano and sax
entwining. The face of our reader, caught in the fiction,
softens. The corners of his mouth turn up
just so. His hand rests on the top of his head.
His hair is silver. Ellington segues to Scott Joplin
to Bernstein. Firelight collects on his glasses.

    He is in the pleasure of fine distinctions and
complicating clauses that match his own parsing of matters.
I want to stroke his cheek, but hesitate to break the spell.
He is both far away, and close enough to heave to
with, "Listen to this!" and "Ohhh. But this!"

and reads paragraphs, whole sections aloud
before he's off again. Or, he fetches up somewhere
in the middle distance wondering at "all these
oversexed characters!" (He reads little new fiction.)
As if in answer, "Rhapsody in Blue" rises up out of the clarinet
crying. But he's back in Rome beside the crinkling fire,
jazz working the room, shingles muffling the rain,
the sounds of a summer afternoon composing themselves
like time and happenstance entering and rippling in a human.

SARAH HANNAH

Some Pacific Vapor

So you think you can bear me, now, do you?
Carry my limp body through centuries
Of sand (soft, made from ground shells, or souls
As some have claimed), likewise, across that blue
That is the paradise-never you deem
We shall inhabit, in which I don cream
And no clothes, or just a muslin dream-come-true
Of a slip on a slip of a girl felled
On a beach, flung faceward into silt, shell,
Seaweed, you can peel me off the dirt
And wake; hold me? I mean really stand it,
Like childbirth or kidney stones (the male
Equivalent, they say); be mine, ocean's
End, not blink or look back, just face the sun.

C. G. HANZLICEK

Dolphin Weather

> *That there is no it, only is.*
> —Richard Ford

Two days ago, the sun
Was a white stone in the leaden sky,
The black-eyed Susans looked up
And fell back wilted, just as I wilted
And retreated to the air conditioner.
Today a breeze has flowed from the northwest,
It's 28 degrees cooler,
And I can almost smell the ocean
Though it has arrived from 200 miles away.
If I let myself go for a moment,
I can see the dolphins,
Three of them in their usual glee,
Scooting upright on their tails in the grass.
On the other side of this breezy joy,
2,000 miles between us, my mother:
My father heart-stopped 30 years ago,
Her friends entered into their final privacy
Or opening the door to it.
I want to go, she says,
What good is looking out this window all day?
A yellow swallowtail butterfly,
Renewed, whiffles around the lilies
Then over the yard, stirs the dog
To earnest, short-of-the-mark leaps:
This dog will hunt.
And wipe drool on my knee when he gives up.
A hummingbird bullets by us,
Chasing another from the feeder;
This territory is worth defending.
How suddenly blue the sky is.

How fond I am of the air itself.
I close my eyes and hear
The dolphins make another pass.

CHRISTIE HODGEN

Tom & Jerry

October

Another night in the hospital and nothing makes sense to you but that yellow-eyed cat, seething, slobbering, Ahab-mad, nightly one a.m., TV38. You are stuck in bed on an intravenous paralytic, so many sites blown, bruised to hell, the nurses have had to work their way up one arm and down another, all of this—the mindless, layabout life of a cat—to keep a baby from coming too soon.

Something to pass the time. Flipping channels and how happy you'd been to see them, cat and mouse, still running in circles around the same old house, Mammy Two Shoes giving chase in her slippers, slapping her broom, just as they'd always done all those years when you'd sat watching cross-legged on the basement floor of your grandmother's house. You'd been delighted to see them in the way people tend to be delighted when they find things unchanged by time. That slavering hunger, that slapdash pursuit, everything just as it was in childhood, the violence as spectacular, as thrilling, as brilliant as fireworks. At first, the fun was in watching the cat take his lumps; now the fun comes in the moments just beforehand, when you sense what is coming but the cat does not, in such moments you feel clairvoyant, superior, you feel the satisfaction of a God watching his subjects make flagrant disasters of their tiny lives. *If only the cat would learn,* you think. *If only he would take instruction.* There are certain laws of motion particular to his universe—there's a certain Murphy's law of gravity operating about his person—that he'd do well to study. Each night, after the show ends, you entertain yourself with the enumeration of these phenomena in a formal letter to the cat.

Dear Tom: you think.

Kindly allow me to fill you in on a few of life's inevitabilities. Believe me, it is for your own good that I warn you: while attempting to smite Jerry with an umbrella you will trip, fall, and swallow said umbrella, it will spring open and distort your face to its shape; all raised piano lids will collapse on your fingers and likewise with kitchen windows; when you launch explosives towards your enemies they will fail to detonate, for unknown reasons you will follow up with them—those red sticks of dynamite, those black balls with hissing wicks—and demand to know their ailments, you will shake them, hold them to your ear, your face will be blasted off; at various times, without your noticing, your own tail will be substituted for other objects, such as hot dogs and cigars, and you will bite down into or set fire to yourself, you will scream the scream of the dying; when launching a bowling ball down a lane, your fingers will, without question stick, in its holes, your entire body will soar through the air and strike down every last pin, you will come tumbling out of the return chute to the delight of your opponents; now and then you will be flattened by anvils falling from great heights and cars traveling at high speeds; as a general rule, every blow to your head will result in the rising of an equal and opposite red welt.

What I am writing to tell you, Dear Tom, is that with a minimal increase in cognizance I believe you'll find these dangers to be entirely avoidable. Really, it is all quite simple.

This is what one does when confined to bed. Like Proust, one lies about making grand philosophies out of other people's suffering. You do this because there is literally nothing else to do. You are four months' pregnant and have gone into preterm labor, you are completely effaced, you have been drugged senseless in an effort to stop contractions, but the efforts are thought to be futile. You are waiting to deliver what you have been told will be a stillborn, or at the very best a baby that will gasp for an hour in your arms before dying, the baby being, in the strictest medical terms, the size of a potato and too small to save: any day now, you're told. The medication you're on is a poison, a chemical compound that has the effect of shutting down your body's functioning and thereby labor. What it feels like is mercury in the veins, an unbearable heaviness, a dozen x-ray aprons piled atop you. You can move, but only slowly and with great effort against a formidable invisible force; you move, that is, like a mime. Side effects include but are not limited to: nausea and vomiting, migraine, profuse sweating, hypotension, arrhythmia, double vision. Possible complications include cardiac arrest, lung failure, profound muscular paralysis, fetal death, maternal death, all of the above. When you were first admitted, it was thought you'd deliver before nightfall. But it has been three weeks. Your life, it seems, has been turned into some loathsome French novel in which, in order to illustrate certain theories of plotlessness, the main character does nothing, absolutely nothing, the main character is so motionless one is left to wonder if she is alive or dead.

Only a month ago, you were a fully functioning human being, a French teacher at a Catholic girls' high school. You had a schedule, a checking account, a small basement apartment you'd appointed to the best of your ability given the limitations of your budget and taste; you had a green bicycle with a wicker basket in which you carried around clothbound library books that hadn't, in most cases, been checked out by a living soul since nineteen fifty-seven; you had a cactus, a goldfish; five days a week and five classes a day you had a profusion of verbs to conjugate aloud, in multiple tenses, in front of dozens of indifferent students; you had a longstanding predilection for the subjunctive; you had an expensive block of Irish cheese in your refrigerator, a pile of unwanted mail, including a jury duty summons, sitting on the kitchen table which doubled as your desk; you had blue eyes and pale, freckled skin; you had a pleasant face, not a beautiful one, more like a beautiful face reflected in a spoon, but still it was something you didn't mind looking at, it was something with which you could get by; you had, in other words, a life, not a great one but yours, it was something.

Now here you are in perpetual pajamas like Hugh Hefner, the absurd protagonist of a dreadful story, cruelly paused just short of the crisis, with nothing to do but wait. Something bad is about to happen and you are waiting, the contractions mounting and quelling, you are waiting, day running into night into day. All the while, people come in and out of your room performing their assigned functions: they roll you to the side and yank down your underpants and administer steroid shots into the flesh of your hip, your hindquarters as it were; they hook new bags fluid to your IV pole—those glistening bags of poison—and set them running; they draw blood; they consult monitors and charts and frown; they take your blood pressure and ask you if you are alive because, they say, according to their calculations you are dead;

every three days, they warm a special bonnet in the microwave and then place it over your head, massage the bonnet with their fingers to activate its inner chemical lining, they tell you this has the same hygienic results as a shower and shampoo, but you're not convinced, like dry cleaning, it seems to you the main talents of the bonnet have to do with fragrance; they settle bedpans underneath you and command you to fill them, they squeeze cold jelly onto your stomach and run sensors across it, they pronounce the estimated weight of the baby at thirteen ounces.

You have to do something to pass the time and so while you wait you watch television, you watch like you used to as a child, which is to say you watch without discrimination, watch with equal interest comedies and dramas and game shows and talk shows and the commercials between them. You watch even the unwatchable—weather conditions reported by the voice of a robot who seems to be speaking from the very back of its robot throat, channels plagued with static, telethons. One of the public broadcasting stations is immersed in its annual fund drive and the stakes, to you, seem as monumental as the Cuban missile crisis. Behind the telecaster (fat, bald, plaid-suited, appealingly pathetic) is a handmade chart in the shape of a thermometer with the raised funds shown in red rising toward the projected goal. The raised funds are pathetically low, the mercury stays sunken in its well, in the background a single telephone rings and is answered, and now the broadcaster has something on his mind, a serious question: whether or not the station you are currently watching will live to see another day or whether it will fold, shut down its signal, send its sad employees home laid-off to their small children, the question to you is, considering how much public television contributes to your life and mind, will you rise to the occasion, will you please help?

On another channel, the question is whether or not you will rise to the aid of Central American orphans. Asking the question are their big, wet eyes and their distended stomachs, asking the question is a slow-motion montage of images, children running barefoot through puddles of sewage and drinking from the same pails as their goats.

On still another channel, the question is whether or not you will contribute your heart, mind, and ten percent gross earnings to the ministry of Dr. Creflo A. Dollar. *Can this really be the name of a televangelist?* you think to yourself. You smirk, you scoff, you take note of his brilliant, shimmering, double-breasted suits, his diamond rings, and you wonder how it is that he manages to convince people, poor people, to send *him* money, he of the polished shoe and silk tie, he of the glistening cufflinks. You laugh—*Ha!*—but only in your head.

You watch all of this as if a stranger to this world looking through its window in the hopes of understanding its inhabitants. You watch and you wait.

The idea is to immerse yourself in something, anything other than the wait itself, which is projected by all experts to end in tragedy, you are waiting for the story to end, waiting to lose your firstborn, as is the fate of all stupid girls in fairytales who, in exchange for good looks and a handsome prince, promise their babies to witches. You are waiting and turning every moment into a narrative. Like Rapunzel, like a spider, like a planet, like a drunk, you are spinning and spinning and endlessly spinning, spinning a tale, constantly a voice runs in your head, translating all that happens to you into the second person. This voice is female, with a slight British accent, like yours but more mellifluous and intelligent; this voice will not shut up, it will not *shut the fuck up* though you keep telling it to and you start to wonder if—no, you're quite sure of this—maniacs live this way, if after only three weeks you have already gone batshit, bonkers, berserk, Howard Hughes crazy, Joan of Fucking Arc crazy, crazy from which there is no return. The voice, it doesn't stop, it simply won't stop.

On the rare occasions when the voice *does* stop it is only because it has been preempted by the voice of Peter Jennings, who breaks in with his own newscast. Once or twice a day, you imagine Peter Jennings reporting your condition from behind his desk, you can see his head cocked slightly, the slender gleam of his tiepin. He says things like: *For those of you tuning in tonight, I am pleased to report that in the case of our favorite patient there has been, as of yet, no delivery. Another day has come and gone and the doctors, working tirelessly around the clock, have managed to quell the contractions once again. As for our patient, she is still drugged into paralysis, but is said to be bearing up admirably. Do we have a live feed?* he asks. *May we see into the room for a moment?* From an aerial view you see the room, a small box with a bed in the middle, with hulking, blinking equipment on either side, you see yourself lying pathetically in bed, you see the wires snaking out from the neck and sleeves of your hospital gown, you see the computer screens crawling with the information fed to them by the wires attached to you, the waves of contractions rolling across, the spikes of the fetal and maternal heartbeats, you see your hair, squid-like in dark tendrils, slick with grease, spread across the pillow, you are lying on one side and holding something in your hand. What could it be? The camera pans in and all comes into focus. What you are doing is staring at the ultrasound picture, the picture of your firstborn in utero. White on black, you see the outline of its skull and belly, you see its nose and lips, its spine, its arms. You see that it has raised its fist to its mouth. The camera pans back again and Peter says: *And so it continues.* He says that he will break into regular programming with any updates. He says good night.

One particular nurse—Edith, your favorite—comes in and out of the room constantly, rustling the cellophane wrappers of popsicles. Always she tells you to eat, though it is true you will only throw it up afterwards (the drug you're hooked up to causes you to vomit on the hour, with the precision of certain geysers), she tells you to eat anyway. "You got," says Edith, fat and black as Hattie McDaniel, with the same gruff voice and the same flair for stealing a scene, "to eat something. Put some meat," she tells you, "on that baby! That baby no bigger than a stick of butter and what your job is is to eat this popsicle whether you like it or not, and the whole mess of others I'm gonna bring you after." Edith is the only nurse kind enough to suggest that this story of yours will end as a fairytale, in the happily ever after. She has a story of her own and tells it loud, tells it from on high, walks in the room mid-sentence already telling it: the story involves a girl, *just like you,* who came in the October prior, *twenty weeks along just like you, whitest of white girls just like you,* a girl who stayed paralyzed in bed for four solid months, stayed unspooked through Halloween and All Saint's Day, stayed gratefully through Thanksgiving, stayed proud through Pearl Harbor Day, stayed rejoicing through Christmas and New Years all the way through the birthday of Dr. Martin Luther King, Jr., stayed all that time and gave birth, finally, to healthy twins, the fattest pinkest twins she's ever seen in all her years on the maternity ward. "That mother," she says one day, "had a positive attitude, and that's what made all the difference. She didn't lay around moping with her back turned to the world, she didn't lay around staring out the window like *some* people. It was a positive attitude that made all the difference, a positive attitude that saved those twins, you ask me I'll tell you."

The twins, the twins, the twins, always and everywhere she talks of those twins. One day she walks in and asks you to guess, go on ahead and guess who you just missed passing by the hallway: the twins come for a visit dressed up in pumpkin suits, the twins gurgling and drooling, the twins by the name of Jaime and David and their mother, who after four months paralyzed was so weak she couldn't turn a door knob but who recovered in no time and recently ran a charitable half-marathon. Every time Edith brings you a Popsicle, she tells you something of those twins and their glorious mother. At the end of Edith's shift your mouth is so rimmed in red you have the smile of a circus clown, of a vampire, you have enough stained wooden sticks to build a scale model of your entire hospital room and the equipment inside it. Also at the end of Edith's shift, you have puked so many times into that clever kidney-shaped plastic bowl, that tiny vomitorium, that you think of consulting the Guinness to see if you have broken a world record.

A social worker comes by, then a psychiatrist. They come separately, but say almost the exact same thing.

"We've noticed," says one.

"It has been brought to our attention," says the other. They both speak this way, in the first person plural, like royalty.

"We've noticed you put yourself on NO VISITOR status."

"It has been brought to our attention that you are alone here."

"And that you aren't speaking."

"We're told you run the television and stare out the window all day, like you're doing now."

"Just staring out at the parking lot. Is that the doctor's parking lot? They sure get special treatment, right next to the front entrance, don't they? Boy."

"The nurses are concerned about you."

"The nurses have mentioned you."

"It's not that they're angry or insulted or anything like that, with your not speaking to them or anyone, not even a single word."
"They're professionals and they can work around any kind of circumstance, even complete silence."
"It's just that they, and we, believe the outcome of your situation can be affected by your state of mind."
"They think—we all think—that you have a better chance of pulling through this, the baby has a better chance, if you reach out for help and companionship."
"We can get you some help, some drugs. You'd be amazed."
"We can arrange for visitors if you like. Volunteers. Most of them teenagers. But sometimes the humane society comes by with puppies. They're clinically proven to lift patient spirits, puppies."
"You just think about it."
"Take your time and think about it."
"Let us know."

Visitors! You decide to allow visitors. Mindy and Cindy, your upstairs neighbors, come to visit. Like you, they are teachers at Sacred Heart Academy for Girls, English and History, like you they are doughy, flaccid people who almost never see the light of day. You have lived below them for several years. Your friendship has been forged on the same complaints: students and their papers, perpetual lack of money, the cruel and impenetrable Sacred Heart administration. When Mindy and Cindy come into they room, they smell of the outdoors, of a delicious arctic breeze. They have snowflakes, bits of the outside world, on the shoulders of their jackets, and what you want to do is lick them, actually lick the snowflakes right off their skin, hair and clothing.
"We called and called!" says Mindy.
"We've been calling your hospital room all day and night for weeks, but you've had your phone turned off."
"And we keep coming by but they haven't let us in!"
"It's been terrible."
"Awful, really."
"The thing is," says Cindy.
"What we don't understand," Mindy says.

"Is that we didn't even know you were pregnant!"

"Here we are your best friends and everything."

"Your only friends."

"And you didn't even tell us."

"Obviously it would have been awkward, an unmarried pregnant woman at a Catholic school."

"But really if anyone should understand that kind of thing—"

"When you stop to think about it, if anyone's going to be sympathetic to an unmarried pregnant woman—"

"It would be the Catholics."

"It should be Catholics."

"Obviously the other teachers aren't very nice."

"They're not exactly *warm* or anything."

"In three years, they've hardly spoken to you."

"You'd think after doing a good job for three years they might, but they don't."

"They've been disapproving of your wardrobe."

"And your hair."

"Too much black, they say."

"They've dropped hints."

"And certainly your not going to mass hasn't helped."

"No, that's been a disappointment to everyone."

"They're old-fashioned, they don't understand how it is today, to be young in a time like this."

"But you'd like to think in a crisis."

"In a crisis, you'd like to think they'd rise to the occasion."

"They haven't replaced you or anything."

"They've just got a substitute. A series of substitutes."

"There's still hope for you, we think."

"Anyway we missed you at work, and then at home, we called and called."

"The police and everything."

"And they called the hospital and told us you were here."

"But you didn't call."

"It made us feel weird."

"Sad, in a way."

"We were so worried."

"And then when we found out you were pregnant we were like..."

"We were like, *Oh my God!*"
"How exciting!"
"But how terrible! Because it's too early."
"And then we figured you didn't want us to know."
"Which we couldn't figure out."
"Because we totally would have been okay with it."
"Totally!"
"Regardless of how we feel about the father."
"That would have been put aside."
"Entirely put to the side."
There is an awkward silence. You can't think of anything to say.
"Otherwise there's no news," says Cindy. "You haven't missed much."
"Except the fish," says Mindy. "Mr. Muckle died."
"Not that we weren't taking good care of him," says Cindy. "My feeling is that it was bound to happen anyway and not really our fault."
"Because you never clean the bowl."
"And you forget to feed it sometimes."
"But we didn't come here to tell you that."
"That's true, we didn't."
"What we more or less came here to say—"
"What we've both been thinking is—"
"Maybe all this trouble you're having—"
"Maybe this whole awful business—"
"Maybe," they say in unison, "it's all for the best."
They kiss you on the forehead. These kinds of gestures don't usually pass between you and you are moved. When they go to leave, you have the urge to claw at the hems of their garments and pull them down with you into your private hell, but of course you don't.

By far the most important part of the day is *Tom & Jerry*, which, like all of your life's past pleasures, you have managed to ruin with obsessive analysis. Lately, you have begun to sympathize with the cat, to suspect that the cat's continued failures are speaking to you personally, you feel now as if the cat's tribulations are mocking reenactments of your own life. Watching him, you feel anxious, wounded, mortified. Most painful are the moments when the cat is walking around satisfied with himself. He has done something clever, he has shut away the mouse deep within a series of nesting suitcases, he has licked clean a saucer full of cream, he has exacted revenge, he has spotted a girl and commanded her attention, he has done any or all of these things and so walks on his hind legs with his chest thrust out. But the problem with the cat's walking like this—as it is for you and likewise all the world—is that in such a position his heart and genitals are exposed, they are right out there tempting some violence, and sure enough it comes calling. At the height of his glory the cat is knocked down in the most humiliating fashion and what hurts to watch is not the fall itself, but the perfect confidence with which the cat carries himself directly into the clutches of certain doom. Watching these scenes over and over, you are moved, you feel in those moments something like the pity and compassion you were always instructed to feel in church but could never muster.

One episode in particular you almost can't make it through. Here Tom is shown in pursuit of his intended. He lugs a string bass to her back yard and plays beneath her bedroom window, plays right there next to the dog house, without regard for peril. He cries up to the lighted window: *Is you is or is you ain't my baby? The way you acting lately makes me doubt.* And the intended comes to the window. She pouts, she blinks, she sighs, she props her chin on her paw, she watches with boredom as Tom is dismembered, utterly torn to pieces by a spike-collared bulldog. *Yes,* you think. *That's just how it went.*

After *Tom & Jerry*, you always turn off the TV and wait for sleep, which doesn't come. You stare out the window conjugating verbs. *Je dormirai*, you say. *Je dormirais. Si je dorme.*

November

Something about the weather, the nurses say, the cycle of the moon combined with a drastic barometric shift, there's a snowstorm, and right in the middle of it the hospital is overflowing with women gone into labor. You hear their cries, you hear the cries of the newly born. Past your door you see them wheeled in beds and chairs and isolettes. One day, a bed is wheeled into your room—what you have come to think of as your own personal room—with a hugely pregnant woman lying on it. She has brown hair, brown eyes, and a freckled face, her hair is done up in braided pigtails, she reminds you of a grown-up Laura from *Little House on the Prairie.*

"It's crazy in here," says Edith, "and we outta room so you two have to be roommates for a bit." As if to prove Edith's point, someone cries out in pain from the next room, and she leaves, leaves you with this new roommate, this pigtailed settler.

"You pregnant?" says the roommate. "You don't look none pregnant."

You nod.

"Watcha in labor or something?"

You shrug.

"I'm three weeks early but it looks like I gone into labor."

You nod.

"Boy you sure did keep your figure," she says. "You're lucky you didn't blow up like a whale like me."

Her name is Amanda and she is determined to tell you her life story in as much painful detail as she can manage to recall, starting, like David Copperfield, at birth. "I was born right here in this here hospital—maybe even in this very room, who knows, that'd be funny, wouldn't it? My momma had me right here, right in this same place if you can believe that." She tells you of her childhood in a trailer park on the edge of town, her brothers and sisters and the trouble they got into vandalizing other trailers, how they slept outside in sleeping bags all summer and how she once rolled her brother, asleep, into a creek, her parents who worked in the dog food factory, her father the day shift and her mother the night. She tells you about her first sex, age thirteen, her first pregnancy at the age of sixteen, how she dropped out of high school and always planned to go back, or at least get her GED, but didn't, the birth of her son—*right here, maybe even right her in this room, I can't remember, but wouldn't that be funny?*—her first son who's eighteen now and just started college, but she can't remember where because when he turned ten he went to live with his Daddy in St. Louis and she hasn't seen him since. "That was right about the time," she says, "when Michael left for his Daddy's, that was right about the time I had my second baby, Dean, who's half-black. Michael always said it didn't make no difference to him, Dean being half-black, but I always thought that's why he left for his Daddy's, he said it was the noise and him not being able to do his school work with a baby in the house, but secretly I always thought it was Dean being half-black, nobody liked it, nobody never said anything but you know how people are, nobody likes a white woman and a black man together, it gives people the willies, who knows why but it does."

After forty solid minutes, she asks you about yourself. But by this time you've rolled away from her. You don't say anything, pretend you're asleep.

"Well," she says. "I didn't know I was in the presence of *greatness* or nothing like that. Sorry to bother you. I didn't know you were thinking all kinds of deep personal thoughts over there. Excuse *me*." She turns on the television, a talk show in which an estranged mother and daughter relay messages of hatred and resentment to one another through the host. "Tell her," says the mother, "she's an ungrateful little monster."

"Well you tell *her*," says the daughter, "she's a pathetic fat cow and to mind her own business."

"I won't bother you anymore," Amanda says. "I'll be quiet over here. Nice and quiet."

On another channel, two drag queens are fighting over a third, relaying messages of hatred and resentment to one another through the host. "Would you please tell her?" says the first drag queen, "that she's a pathetic fat cow?"

"Well you tell *her*," says the second, "she's an ungrateful little monster."

"I think," Amanda says, "those are men." She shuts off the TV and sighs, then sighs again. "Well we gotta pass the time *somehow*," she says. "I'm alone like you. Ain't nobody come here to visit me. My boyfriend? Jimmy? He works construction and he don't get off 'til seven. By the time he gets home, he's so tired he just passes right out. He ain't good for nothing when he gets home. He just comes on home and clean passes out on the couch, ain't nothing can wake him. You could hit him with a hammer and he wouldn't even flinch, I swear it. One time me and my friends, we did him all up in lipstick and eyeshadow and he didn't even notice, he just got up in the morning and went on into work like that, I swear."

She picks up the phone—she isn't on bed rest and can do whatever she wants—and calls Jimmy at his apartment but he doesn't answer. "I bet he done passed out already," she says, "once he falls asleep ain't nothing can wake him. I bet you anything I go into labor and he sleeps through the whole thing, you wait and see." She tries to call her twelve-year-old son, Dean, home alone with no one there to watch him, probably drunk and truant from school. "I'd have Jimmy watch him, but he and Dean don't get along none," she says. "Jimmy won't have nothing to do with Dean, that's why me and Jimmy don't live together. He says it's cause Dean's a brat, but I think it's because Dean's half-black and Jimmy don't like blacks for nothing. I do. I don't see no difference black or white or half-black or Chinese or whatever, but some people do, most people do, which is why it's hard for me and Dean to make friends, him being half-black and people being able to tell by looking at him I slept with a black person." Never, never, never does she speak his name without including the phrase "half-black," as in: *My son? Dean? The half-black one?* That phrase, *half-black, half-black, half-black* going around him all his life, attached to him in the prefix and suffix, *half-black Dean, Dean-who's half-black, my half-black son Dean who's half-black, bless his heart.*

"Well he's probably over at the neighbor's," she says. "The neighbor got a boy who's retarded and him and Dean stick together, they get along real good because they ain't got no other friends; they're both outsiders on account of Sam being a retard and Dean being half-black and all."

You can't think of anything to say to this, but it doesn't matter. "After the baby comes me and Jimmy gonna get married. We got rings picked out on layaway, real pretty rings on layaway."

Peter Jennings breaks in. *A new development tonight,* he says, *is putting a strain on our young heroine. Tonight it seems as if the Gods have seen fit to pair her with a roommate scientifically calculated to violate every last one of her sensibilities. As some of you may know she is a person of few words who believes in carrying around her thoughts and experiences deep in the privacy of her own mind. Now she is literally trapped in a room with a person of the exact opposite temperament. Do we have a feed?* he says. You see the room from above, you lying with your back turned to Amanda, looking out the window as always. Into the phone, Amanda is saying, "Thank God you answered. They got me stuck in a room with this roommate who doesn't talk? I mean here I am with nothing to pass the time and I get Quiet McChurchmouse over here, won't say two words for nothing, I swear." She laughs. "Quiet McChurchmouse!" she says.

Amanda stays, talking constantly, for eight days. She rings the call button like a contestant on *Jeopardy!*, keeps it in her hand, calls and calls and calls the nurses, calls them not ten seconds apart, calls and asks them through the intercom: "Can you bring me a Coke? Can you bring me a ham sandwich with a little mustard? Can you bring me just a little more mustard? Can you bring me some chips, some pretzels, some of them twisty cheesy pouffy things? What about a milkshake? Can somebody wheel me outside so I can have a smoke? Would you get me one of them wet wipes? You got any Mylanta, any Tums, any orange-flavor Metamucil? What about Oxycontin, you got any of that? Got any cough syrup with codeine? Extended-release ibuprofen? Gum, at least, you got any gum?" She simply won't kick over into active labor. The nurses keep trying to send her home, but as soon as they get together the paperwork she claims to be afflicted with some grievous ailment. "I can't feel nothing in my left leg," she tells them, "nothing at all, and my right foot is tingling like crazy. I think I might be having a stroke or something. Can someone get me a Coke?"

The worst part is that unlike you, Amanda sleeps at night and so you can't watch *Tom & Jerry*. You watch the clock, 12:30, 12:45, 12:57, and finally one a.m. You wonder which episode is playing. You hear the theme song in your head, all those horns and strings. You feel better just thinking about them.

Every night, well after Amanda is asleep, an old Volvo wagon pulls into a space in the doctor's lot just outside your window. Since the blizzard there has been, perched on the roof of the Volvo, a snowman, complete with stick arms and a carrot nose, complete with a striped scarf. The doctor who owns the car always looks to be in a tremendous hurry. He slams the door and runs for the entrance, his white coat flapping behind him like the cape of a superhero. You like this doctor very much. You like to think of his life, of the kid who looked at him and said, "Hey Dad, can we make a snowman on the roof of your car?" and him saying no at first, thinking of the technical difficulties, and the embarrassment of riding around like that, but then thinking to himself, "Why the hell not?" You like to think you'd be the same, the same kind of parent.

"You awake?" Amanda says one night, "cause I feel like talking." You roll toward her.

"I just wish my momma and daddy were here is all," she says. "I wish they was here to see Kyle when he gets born. I picked the name Kyle myself. It's classy. What you gonna name your kid?"

You speak to her for the first time. You tell her the names you're thinking of—this is the first time you've spoken them out loud—and she bursts into sobs. At first you don't know what has happened but what has happened, apparently, is this: you have just spoken the names of her dead parents. "It's a sign!" she says. "It's a miracle. Those names right there are the names of my dead parents, my momma's dead of breast cancer and my father, he killed himself, but those were their exact names, and what this is is a sign, it's them speaking to me through you and telling me they're here. And right now from this moment." She stops to blow her nose, here, on her bed sheet. "You and me are sisters and you and me are gonna be friends forever, I knew it the minute I saw you!"

Your parents are dead, too, you remember them vaguely, they died drunk in a car crash when you were six, they died and left you to your grandparents, your grandmother who wore handmade smock dresses that buttoned down the center, who went around the house and neighborhood in her slippers and curlers, your grandmother who, when people stopped her on the street to speak of her misfortune—of her having to raise a child again just when she should have been resting, after a lifetime of working and raising kids of her own here she was with another one—always said to them, in a fierce whisper: *I try not to let her know it, but I can't keep up with her much longer, I'm too old and she's too much for me, no I can't keep up. Luckily she has a fine imagination, she plays by herself, she has two little girlfriends, imaginary girlfriends with rhyming names I forget what they are, she certainly entertains herself which is nice, she sits quiet down in the basement in front of the television and has tea parties with those two little girls in her head, I forget their names, but they rhyme, and most days she's quiet as a mouse and you can't even tell she's there.* When you think of those years, you think only of the television, that animated universe, its songs, its glare, the people on it enjoying their lives and how you watched them as if trying to decode something, as if trying to pick some kind of lock, yes, your parents are dead too, all your life you have been alone, this business in the hospital, this not talking to anyone, this isn't out of the ordinary at all, this isn't a muteness brought on by trauma, this is pretty much who you are all the time, with a single extraordinary exception, you have been alone your whole life, but you don't tell her this. You keep this, as everything, to yourself.

Edith comes in and out delivering Amanda's food. "Guess who just came by in little Pilgrim outfits?' she asks you one day. "Guess who showed up dressed like Pilgrims, looking fat as turkeys, so juicy and plump I'd like to stick some paper socks on their feet and roast them in a pan, pull them out the oven from time to time and baste them? Guess who just came by in little black coats and hats, little patent leather belts and boots and suchlike?"

"Who?" says Amanda. "Who?"

The day before Thanksgiving Amanda goes into active labor—that morning she gets up to use the bathroom and says, "Well, shit! My water broke!," and she is taken away, wheeled off. By now you have lost all sense of time and it seems to you that as soon as she leaves she turns right around and comes back carrying a baby, although she tells you later that two days have passed and she is on her way home. This child, too, is half-black, the lovely color of an almond, with a full head of curly hair. "This here is Kyle," she says. "Turns out he weren't Jimmy's after all. I knew it was either one or the other," she says. "Jimmy didn't take the news too good." She tells you how Jimmy, miraculously roused from his nightly coma, had made it to the hospital just in time for the birth, just in time to see for himself the face of the baby he thought was his but plainly wasn't. She tells you how she called him and called him, tried to work things out, but *he wasn't about to have none of it,* no, Jimmy has already packed his things and struck out to make his living in the Alaskan canneries. She hands you the baby—there is some difficulty with the wires but you manage—and you hold him tight. You regard his hands, so small, so impossibly small, tucked under his chin. His eyes are pressed shut. He squirms, he moves his tiny mouth. "Kyle's Daddy," Amanda says, "I don't even remember his name, I was drunk and don't remember nothing about him practically except he was real good looking and of course he was black." She sighs. "I guess those wedding rings just gonna sit there on layaway until they figure out we're not coming." You hold Kyle a long time, longer than necessary or reasonable, you stare into his fat face, you think: *Maybe I'll just keep him. Maybe I'll hold him a while on a layaway plan. Maybe she'll just leave him to me.* For several whole minutes you actually think this. Finally Amanda takes him away—she is suddenly in a great hurry to leave. "Good luck and all," she says. She props the baby on her shoulder and as she walks out the door you watch his face, bunched in pain, you watch him and think: *Kyle, you're fucked.*

That night Tom and Jerry continue to clobber each other's brains out, Tom occasionally getting the best of Jerry but never, never in the end. *Most of all I relate to the cat,* you think, *because of its desperate yearning for what it cannot have.* Time and again you watch him, crazed with hunger, pass up a perfectly good meal in pursuit of the one meal he is forbidden. Time and again he goes mad with rage, the thing he most wants just, just out of reach. He thrusts his arm into Jerry's mouse hole, he slaps his fat white paws around, he crushes flat Jerry's dining set, knocks from Jerry's mouse walls the oval silhouette portraits of his mouse parents, he demolishes Jerry's clever bed, made of four matches and their box, but he never gets what he truly wants. Often in the course of his chase he is cast from his home, Mammy Two Shoes calling from the kitchen: "One more breaking and you is out, O-U-T, Out!" It is sad to watch. *Dear Tom,* you think. *Aretez-vous. Please, please stop.*

December

By now people around the hospital have begun to take notice of your situation. Something extraordinary is happening and it is happening to you. Nurses who initially wanted nothing to do with you—you were clearly just another sad case, another mother to be sent home empty-handed—start to linger. They tell you about their own pregnancies, their own children. They produce photographs from their pocketbooks, children of various ages, each a stereoisomer of its mother. Your baby is now twenty-nine weeks gestation, has a decent chance of survival. The neonatologist comes by for a chat. He tells you that one does not worry about death at this point so much as blindness, paralysis, retardation, heart and lung problems, bleeding in the brain, weeks upon weeks in intensive care, years of medication and physical therapy. He speaks of these things in a bright, high voice. These things are manageable! These things are better than nothing! A child of this sort amounts to a consolation prize, but still it is better than nothing!

Edith comes by one afternoon, laughing, to tell you about a rumor she heard. "They're saying," she tells you, and stops to laugh—*Ha! Woooh!*—"they're saying around here you're some kind of religious figure. You know with the baby staying in there all this time even with no medical reason it should be, what they're saying is," she stops to laugh again—*Ha!*—"what they're saying is you're some kind of martyr or saint-like figure." You smirk. A corner of your mouth turns up. This is the closest you've come to smiling in months. "I *knew*," Edith says, "you'd get a kick out of that one."

A nun stops by from Sacred Heart, the retired headmistress. Her name is Sister Isabelle and you have been together in the same room on several prior occasions, but have never actually met. She has a large mole on her chin, a brown mole in the shape of Florida, and you have often wondered—you are the kind of petty person who wonders about these things—if in fact she joined the convent because of the mole, because of the dark shadow it cast on her any hope of love or marriage. She tells you that word has gotten out, she has been told by several people of your situation and now of the miracle surrounding it, and she believes, she says, that God is going about his strange work in this room at the end of the hall. She presses her palm against your forehead. *All is forgiven you*, she says. She is in full habit—wimple and all!—robed head to toe in black. She is old, trembling old, her face wrinkled as seersucker. For a long moment, she stands with her hand pressed to your forehead as if by doing so she might read your mind. *No*, she says. *You are not alone.* Now one of her hands is on your head and one on your stomach, and you feel something coursing through you, some kind of electricity. A light, a yellow light, absolutely fills the room, so bright you have to close your eyes. You are warm, warm, warmer than you have ever been. *A miracle is happening here,* says the nun. The baby, which almost never moves because it is drugged into the same kind of paralysis you are, rolls over. And lo, she says, *they were sore afraid.* She says, *Be still.*

You have never in your adult life cried in front of another person and won't do it now—no, you won't, you won't, you won't do it, you look away, look out the window.

After that moment—so bizarre you can't think of the words to describe it, Peter Goddamned Jennings can't even think of the words—everything changes. You, even you, start to believe that something extraordinary might happen. You start to think that you have been transformed, converted, rescued from the lonely person you have always been and brought into the fold of humanity. One day you happen again upon the ministry of Dr. Creflo Dollar, and instead of flipping past him, you stay. Then he points his finger directly at you and speaks the word *longsuffering.* His message is this: that life is difficult, that life requires of you a never-ending series of sacrifices and offers in return but meager restitution and sometimes not even that, that we are as a human population essentially rode hard and put away wet—here the crowd before him claps and howls, springs to its feet, they raise their hands in the air as a means of testifying, of bearing witness, they shout *Amen,* someone cries out *Tell it!* and Dr. Creflo A. Dollar tells you that your longsuffering will one day be rewarded, that this life and its agonies are nothing compared with the life of the world to come, nothing, nothing, not a single thing can happen to you in this life that won't be made good later, and already you find yourself nodding, already you find swelling in your chest a fiery emotion you can't name, if you could sit up you would, if you could shout you would, if you could dial a phone and state the numbers of your credit card, you would.

One night, Amanda calls from home. In the background you hear Kyle screaming, screaming his half-black lungs out. "He's got colic," she says. "He won't stop screaming for nothing." She asks you to come over. You tell her you can't right now and she says, "Oh yeah, I forgot, it's just that I didn't want to be alone tonight. I'm so glad we're sisters," she says, "because you can call up your sister any time of the day or night and it's okay, it's just what family does, and family shouldn't never be alone on a night like tonight." Through the window, you see the Volvo drive up. The snowman is still on its roof, but its arms have fallen off and someone has done something obscene with the carrot. Amanda is saying something, but you only catch the end of it. "Tonight of all nights," she says. Only later, when channel 38 runs a *Tom & Jerry* Christmas episode, does it occur to you that it is Christmas Eve.

In this episode, Tom and Jerry have their usual fight. Tom casts Jerry out into the snow but then, in the spirit of Christmas, lets him back into the house. They shake hands. *Maybe*, you think, *it just might be possible*.

Days pass, a week. On New Year's Eve, your IV pops out. You've blown another vein and you need to place a new line before the magnesium wears off and you kick into labor. It is seven o'clock, the end of Edith's shift, and she stops by to find a vein. Unlike the other nurses, she always warms up your arm with a hot cloth before sticking you, and this makes all the difference. "I wish you could have seen those twins in they Santa suits," she says. "Little fur-trimmed coats, little hats, little patent-leather boots, shaking those bellies like little bowls full of jelly. It was something else."

You look at her, look her in the eye. She sticks you, gets the IV running again, tapes it down, flicks the bag with her finger. "I'll see you tomorrow," she says. "Don't go nowhere." A little joke between you.

Whenever you blow a vein, they reload you on a double dose, a bolus. Someone is supposed to come by in an hour and dial you down to a regular dose, but that night no one does. You lie there you know not how long. By this stage of the game, you have been on the paralytic so long you hardly take notice its effects. Sometimes you can move and sometimes you can't, from day to day you feel more, or less, trapped under a pile of stones like Giles Corey, your breathing is more difficult or less from hour to hour, you have gotten so used to these things that you don't notice, that night, for a while, you simply don't notice that you have crossed over into another territory altogether, that you can't move and that your heart is doing something it has never done before, it seems to be flapping in your chest like a bird attempting flight. When it *does* hit you, the fact that something has gone very wrong, you try to move your arm toward the call button, which you can see but can't reach—true paralysis has set in, your arm won't work, you lie there staring at it—you try to call out but can't so much as open your mouth. You struggle with these things—these most basic of tasks—for quite some time. You realize that your fate, the baby's fate, depends on the off chance that someone comes to check on you. But from all your nights awake—how many of them, now?—you know that one ever does, no one will.

You stare out the window at the falling snow. You think of Robert Frost and his promises left to keep, the poem you were made to memorize in third grade. You remember Mrs. Smith trying to explain the repetition of the last line: *and miles to go before I sleep*. This repetition, she claimed, was no matter of the poet running out of things to say and so therefore saying the same thing twice, no, you were all quite wrong about that. Rather it was meant to suggest that our tired traveler was giving in, that he was about to fall prey to the woods, lovely dark and deep, that he would freeze to death in their midst. You can just make out the monitors to the side of the bed, your heart rate making only the faintest spikes and the same with the baby's, in fact it seems to you that the baby's line is flat—you keep watching it and sometimes it seems okay and others it doesn't, your vision is blurred and it's hard to tell, you just can't tell, but what you know for a fact, what you know absolutely, is that if the baby is gone there is nothing left to live for. These months here have, you realize, meant something, in fact the act of lying still, of doing nothing, for the sake of another person, your child, all these months of nothing have amounted to the greatest trial and triumph of your life, these months you have been closer to someone than you have ever been before, and if, at the end of this, the baby is gone, then there is nothing left to live for indeed. This is what you're thinking when everything goes quiet. A quiet comes over you such as you've never known before, you can't see or hear or feel anything, for a long moment you are just floating, and then you are dead.

You die! For a few minutes you are actually dead! There is a break in the narrative. An alarm sounds. People come in the dark to do their desperate, frantic work, like stagehands changing scenery, they come with the crash cart, they work your chest, all of this happens unbeknownst to you because as mentioned previously you have ceased to live. You are quite offstage.

Peter Jennings interrupts the regularly scheduled programming to report your death. *Sad news tonight,* he says, his voice slow and heavy. His shirt is rumpled, his tie loose, even his impeccable hair is mussed. He has been sitting behind the news desk, constantly sitting there, for weeks now and your story has taken its toll on him, too. He is heartbroken, anyone can see this, anyone can see that he wants to go home and take a hot shower and sleep for a month and a half.

The next day, having been brought back to life, you wake to find Edith standing over you. Her hand rests on your heart. You open your eyes and close them, open them again.

"You just rest," says Edith. You do. You start to drift off but you can still feel her hand on your chest. As yet you have no memory of the night before and you fall into a peaceful half-sleep. But then Edith says something that wakes you up, wakes you terribly and completely. "I never seen," she says, "a girl suffer long as you."

And you're back in it.

A question forms in your mind, a series of questions. What you want to know is plain and simple. What you want to know is elaborate and difficult. You want to know if the baby made it through. You want to know if, after all this time, you have lost it in the end. Your plans—the things you have dared to dream about these last weeks, how you'd have the baby and hold it, how you'd bring it home and love it—you want to know if these things are still possible. You want to know something of your hopes concerning the man you've loved for years—the man you followed west to graduate school and waited around for, six years now, the man who was always going back and forth, loving you and then not, calling you over and then sending you home, the only man you've ever loved. Because he was difficult, because he was troubled, because he was alone, too, and always had been, you had loved him for this and loved him still even when he sent you away, pregnant this last time, you'd *still* believed he would come around in the end. What you want to know is: your hopes involving the baby, and its father, are they still possible? You want to know if you are alone now, alone again, this time more alone than you have ever been. You want to know what Edith meant—what did she mean when she said she'd never seen this before, never seen anyone suffer so long? You want to know all of this, but it tangles in your mind and the only think you can think to say is this: "What about that other girl," you say, "just like me, what about her, the one with the twins, just like me?"

You look into Edith's eyes, lovely dark and deep, you look into them and have your answer even before she speaks, in that moment you realize your mistake, all is revealed to you then, what a fool you are, what a fool you have always been and ever will be, you know all of this even before she says: *Oh, honey. Weren't no girl. Weren't never no girl like that.*

BOB HICOK

My stab at recruiting

The all volunteer
unarmored drop-out
meth-head accepting
army, be all

you can be dead
here and slow or swifter
in the sand, poor black
white chicanas

need jobs, who doesn't
like bread
with their shrapnel
in the morning, I feel

a draft coming, a daft
numbing of sense,
can you dig it,
your fox hole

ain't foxy, mama
don't let your babies
John Hancock
for the man, you

the man, I the man,
all this manliness
gets you in the shit
and shit-canned, IED

deceased or pushing up,
is it the strip-teasing
of daisies tells us
deploy me, re-deploy me

not or Congress, an act of,
enact love in what you do
and don't shoot
until you see the rights

of their eyes
to have it, life
liberty and the pursuit of,
I don't know, breath, more fiber.

TONY HOAGLAND

Powers

There is something clean and complete about autumn.
The ground looks swept under the trees.
The light has the quality of a mild detergent.
And the mailman walks down the street whistling,
sorting the Bills from the Janes.

Now the convulsions of feeling are over.
Summer has yielded its powers in exchange for peace.
The sun sets like an old commodities trader.
The artist begins to study the art of subtraction.

Turns out the real reason for growing up
was to learn what to do with suffering.
Not acting surprised was the answer.
What else do you want to know?

In the grass energy and matter continue their conversation.
Clouds brood on the horizon
From somewhere a radio speaks
of terrible things in the distance.

But Sweetheart, haven't we had our hours of love?
Our dazzling moments of truth-in-speech?
What are we but monkeys who have learned to drive cars,
who have the freedom to read or not to read Proust?

On the marquee this week, I see
the movie about superheroes is here:
Flame Girl who throws fireballs at crime.
Elastic Man who stretches like a rubberband.
Kid Rock with the bulletproof skin.

Our powers are slightly different from theirs, it's true:
but you have the ability
              never to seem in a hurry;
and mine, mine is the invincible human power
                        to remain perpetually amused.

COLETTE INEZ

Looking for Nana in Virginia

She's in the purple cone flowers,
in the yarrow turning brown,
nodding to lemon lilies.
I hear her slighting a neighbor:
"She's flat as an ironing board."
Nana hands me an iron.
"Get your head out of those books,
they'll fill you up with words."
She's in my word pie, my alphabet soup.
The day she died broke the record
of a hundred degrees.
The sun a cooked squash,
her long-boned horny feet stuck out of the sheet.
I thought nothing was uglier than old,
crisscrossed skin, thin ridged lips.
Nana says nothing makes her sick
when I offer a kiss from this world to the next,
and the amaryllis lifts its throat to bees,
to cabbage butterflies, and I slip into words,
what they mean when they come, at last,
to taste me with their tongues.

What the Air Takes Away

"Someone stole my name," a girl sobs,
pigtails cinched with
blue rubber bands.
I want to name the bus
we wait for, Huff, the wind, What?
Inferno, sigh the fried potatoes
whose scent drifts in from a luncheonette.
Who stole the land where potatoes first were sown?
Who stole the vernacular of ancestors?
And that lost father?
I name him flute-wielder, a runner after
fire too-soon-gone-out.
I name him toad-filling-the-night-with-calls.
If I wept in the Quechua or Tzotzil tongues,
these metaphors might sing
to the goddess of names who offers
her shoulder to the child
that she may endure the departure
of her father's voice, inaudible as "b"
in numb, gone, invisibly gray like an empty bus
in a white glare of sky gathering snow.

ROY JACOBSTEIN

Black

Ann Arbor V.A. Hospital

Black matter, black hole, blacker
than charcoal, tar, crow in winter,
blackest thing I'd ever seen,
thirty years later the blackest thing
I've ever seen, that thin black leg
below the still-white thigh angling
from the veteran's hospital gown
the way person, place and time
long ago angled away from his grip.
And all they wanted, his family
up from Kentucky to see him
through the A-K amputation
meant to halt the gangrene's advance,
was for us to give him (under
their breath they asked, hushed plea
at the end of the medical history
taken from those who could give it,
at the end of his story of service
at Leyte, Guam, Guadalcanal, return
to the slag pits, migration to the tool-
and-die shops of Ypsilanti, wife
and three kids, then the gradual total
surrender of any and all) "a little extra."
But I was just the first-year student,
my white coat short, deferment long,
and I didn't know enough to say yes.

MARK JARMAN

Fates at Baptist Hospital

A Godly life would be the best,
If it could be lived, so would Eden,
If we had stayed there.
Meanwhile we can choose a Godly life.

For Eden is still burning,
And the air scorches our lungs,
Our tongues, our young, and yet,
Another Eden remains a possibility.

To live for others,
To pray without pause,
To dedicate the waking hours
To heaven...

So I was thinking after my doctor's visit
And the tests and the reassuring conversation
In his office and the making
Of another appointment.

On the hospital elevator three women joined me,
Laughing, as one, the pretty one, sneezed,
The loudest, pumpkin plump with moles,
Cackled and teased her, and one,

A tattered coat upon a stick, said, "Y'all cut it out!"—
Conspiratorial, like Nörns, with no idea
That I sensed who they were,
Nor interest in me.

And I was thinking about the Godly life,
And how eternity might feel,
And yet, in their company,
Knew I was happy.

I found my car in the garage below
An image of a bunch of grapes—no letter,
No number—and felt lucky then
To be still in one piece.

Haiku

Things that can turn to shrapnel:
Steel and stone. Crockery.
Wood. Glass. And bone.

TED KOOSER

110th Birthday

Helen Stetter

Born into an age of horse-drawn wagons
that knocked and rocked over rutted mud
in the hot wake of straw, manure and flies,
today she glides to her birthday party
in a chair with sparkling carriage wheels,
along a lane of smooth gray carpeting
that doesn't jar one petal of the corsage
pinned to her breast. Her hair is both light
and light as milkweed down, and her chin
thrusts forward into the steady breezes
out of the next year, and the next and next.
Her eyelids, thin as old lace curtains,
Are drawn over dreams, and her fingers
move only a little, touching what happens
next, no more than a breath away. Her feet,
in fuchsia bedroom slippers, ride inches above
the world's hard surface, up where she belongs,
safe from the news, and now and then, as if
with secret pleasure, she bunches her toes
the way a girl would, barefoot in sand
along the Niobrara, just a century ago.

Theater Curtains

A row of lights behind the valence
lets down warm loops of plummy color,
matte with dust, but even in light,
deep folds of shadow stand like a forest,
hiding the whispering players. We
of the audience chatter and shift
as we wait for the curtains to open,
keeping our eyes on the empty apron,
its surface scuffed by the borrowed shoes
of a thousand illusions. Above,
in the loops of light, the motes sift loose
and, snow-like, float from the velvet
into the darkness under the rafters,
as if an old applause were reassembling
the sounds of its separate hands.

Writing Paper

That's what my mother called
her dimestore pads of Irish Linen,

each sheet with its trace of red gum
threaded along the top, thumbed off

for elegance. For special, she'd say,
to be used for letters, not lists,

to be used to write about the weather
one day at a time. But she got

only partway through her last pad,
with its sheet after sheet of good

intentions, before all of her friends
were swept beyond the reach

of a postage stamp, and then she too
was taken, leaving a faint impression

from her dried-out, ten cent ballpoint:
Dear Theresa. Not much new.

WILLIAM LYCHACK

Stolpestad

Was toward the end of your shift, a Saturday, another one of those long slow lazy afternoons of summer—sun never burning through the clouds, clouds never breaking into rain—the odometer like a clock ticking all these bored little pent-up streets and mills and tenements away. The coffee shops, the liquor stores, laundromats, police, fire, gas stations to pass—this is your life, Stolpestad—all the turns you could make in your sleep, the brickwork and shop fronts and river with its stink of carp and chokeweed, the hills swinging up free from town, all momentum and mood, roads smooth and empty, this big blue hum of cruiser past houses and lawns and long screens of trees, trees cutting open to farms and fields all contoured and high with corn, air thick and silvery, as if something was on fire somewhere—still with us?

The sandy turnaround—always a question, isn't it?

Gonna pull over and ride back down or not?

End of your shift—or nearly so—and in comes the call over the radio. It's Phyllis, dispatcher for the weekend, and she's sorry for doing this to you, but a boy's just phoned for help with a dog. And what's she think you look like now, you ask, town dogcatcher? Oh, you should be so lucky, she says and gives the address and away we go.

No siren, no speeding, just a calm quiet spin around to this kid and his dog, back to all the turns you were born, your whole life spent along the same sad streets. It has nothing to do with this story, but there are days you idle slow and lawful past these houses as if to glimpse someone or something—yourself as a boy, perhaps—the apartments stacked with porches, the phone poles and wires and sidewalks all close and cluttered, this woman at the curb as you pull up and step out of the cruiser.

Everything gets a little worse from here, the boy running out of the brush in back before you so much as say hello. He's what— eight or nine years old—skinny kid cutting straight to his mother.

Presses himself to her side, catches his breath, his eyes going from you to your uniform, your duty belt, the mother trying to explain what happened and where she is now, the dog, the tall grass, behind the garage, she's pointing. And the boy—he's already edging away from his mother—little stutter steps and the kid's halfway around the house to take you to the animal, his mother staying by the side porch as you follow toward the garage and garbage barrels out back, you and the boy wading out into the grass and scrub weeds, the sumac, the old tires, empty bottles, paint cans, rusted car axle, refrigerator door. Few more steps and there—small fox-colored dog—lying in the grass, a beagle mix, as good as sleeping at the boy's feet, that vertigo buzz of insects rising and falling in the heat, air thick as a towel over your mouth.

And you stand there and wait—just wait—and keep waiting, the boy not saying a word, not looking away from the dog, not doing anything except kneeling next to the animal, her legs twisted awkward behind her, the grass tamped into a kind of nest where he must have squatted next to her, where this boy must have talked to her, tried to soothe her, tell her everything was all right. There's a steel cooking pot to one side—water he must have carried from the kitchen—and in the quiet the boy pulls a long stem of grass and begins to tap at the dog. The length of her muzzle, the outline of her chin, her nose, her ear—it's like he's drawing her with the brush of grass—and as you stand there, he pushes the feather top of grass into the corner of her eye. It's a streak of cruel he must have learned from someone, the boy pushing the stem, pressing it on her until, finally, the dog's eye opens as black and shining as glass. She bares her teeth at him, the boy painting her tongue with the tip of grass, his fingers catching the tags at her throat, sound like ice in a drink.

And it's work to stay quiet, isn't it? A real job to let nothing happen, to just look away at the sky, to see the trees, the garage beyond, the dog again, the nest of grass, this kid brushing the grain of her face, the dog's mouth pulled back, quick breaths in her belly. Hours you stand there—days—standing there still now, aren't you?

And when he glances up to you, his chin is about to crumble, the boy about to disappear at the slightest touch, his face pale and raw and ashy, scoured-looking. Down to one knee next to him— and you're going to have to shoot this dog—you both must realize this by now, the way she can't seem to move, her legs like rags, that sausage link of intestine under her. The boy leans forward and sweeps an ant off the dog's shoulder.

God knows you don't mean to try to chatter this kid into feeling better, but when he turns, you press your lips into a line and smile and ask him what her name is. He turns to the dog again—and again you wait—wait and watch this kid squatting hunch-curved next to the dog, your legs going needles and nails under you, the kid's head a strange whorl of hair as you hover above him, far above this boy, this dog, this nest, this field. And when he glances to you, it's a spell he's breaking, all of this about to become real with her name—Goliath—but we call her Gully for short, he says.

And you ask if she's his dog.

And the boy nods—mine and my father's, he says.

And you go to one knee, touch your hand to the grass, ask the boy how old he is.

And he says nine.

And what grade is nine again?

Third.

The dog's eyes are closed again when you look—bits of straw on her nose, her teeth yellow, strands of snot on her tongue—nothing moving until you stand up and kick the blood back into your legs, afternoon turning to evening, everything going grainy in the light. The boy dips his hand in the cooking pot and tries to give water to the dog with his fingers, sprinkling her face, her mouth.

A moment passes—and then another—and soon you're brushing the dust from your knee and saying, C'mon—let's get back to your mother, before she starts to worry.

She appears out of the house as you approach—out of the side door on the steps as you and the boy cross the lawn—boy straight to her side once again, his mother drawing him close, asking was everything okay out there. And neither of you say anything—everyone must see what's coming—if you're standing anywhere near this yard you have to know that sooner or later she's going to ask if you can put this dog down for them. She'll ask if you'd like some water or lemonade, if you'd like to sit a minute, and you'll thank her and say no and shift your weight from one leg to the other, the woman asking what you think they should do.

Maybe you'll take that glass of water after all, you say—the boy sent into the house—the woman asking if you won't just help them. Doesn't she want to call a vet?

No, she tells you—the boy pushing out of the house with a glass of water for you—you thanking him and taking a good long drink, the taste cool and metallic, the woman with the boy at her side, her hand on the boy's shoulder, both of them stiff as you hand the glass back and say thank you again.

A deep breath and you ask the woman if she has a shovel. To help bury the dog, you say.

She unstiffens slightly, says she'd rather the boy and his father do that when he gets home from work.

In a duffel in the trunk of the cruiser is an automatic—an M9—and you swap your service revolver for this Beretta of yours. No discharge, no paperwork, nothing official to report, the boy staying with his mother as you cross the yard to the brush and tall weeds in back, grasshoppers spurting up and away from you, dog smaller when you find her, as if she's melting, lying there, grass tamped in that same nest around her, animal as smooth as suede. A nudge with the toe of your shoe and she doesn't move—you standing over her with this hope that she's already dead—that shrill of insects in the heat and grass as you nudge her again. You push until she comes to life, her eye opening slow and black to you—you with this hope that the boy will be running any moment to you now, hollering for you to stop—and again the work of holding still and listening.

Hey, girl, you say and release the safety of the gun. You bend at the waist and gently touch the sight to just above the dog's ear, hold it there, picture how the boy will have to find her—how they're going to hear the shots, how they're waiting, their breaths held—and you slide the barrel to the dog's neck, to just under the collar, the wounds hidden as you squeeze one sharp crack, and then another, into the animal.

You know the loop from here—the mills, the tenements, the streetlights flickering on in the dusk—and still it's the long way around home, isn't it? Wife and pair of boys waiting dinner for you, hundred reasons to go straight to them, but soon you're an hour away, buying a sandwich from a vending machine, calling Sheila from a payphone to say you're running a little late. Another hour back to town, slow and lawful, windows open, night plush and cool, roads a smooth hum back through town for a quick stop at The Elks, couple of drinks turning into a few—you know the kind of night—same old crew at the bar playing cribbage, talking Yankees, Red Sox, this little dog they heard about, ha, ha, ha. Explain how word gets around, ha, ha, ha—how you gave the pooch a blindfold and cigarette, ha, ha, ha—another round for everyone, ha, ha, ha—three cheers for Gully—the next thing you know being eleven o'clock and the phone behind the bar for you.

It's Sheila—and she's saying someone's at the house, a man and a boy on the porch for you—be right there, you tell her. Joey asks if you want one for the road as you hand the receiver over the bar, and you drink this last one standing up, say goodnight, and push yourself out the door to the parking lot, the darkness cool and clear as water, the sky scattershot with stars. And as you stand by the car and open your pants and piss half-drunk against that hollow drum of the fender, it's like you've never seen stars before, the sky some holy-shit vastness all of a sudden, you gazing your bladder empty, staring out as if the stars were suns in the black distance.

It's not a dream—though it often feels like one—the streets rivering you home through the night and the dark, the déjà vu of a pickup truck in the driveway as you pull around to the house, as if you've seen or imagined or been through all of this before, or will be through it all again, over and over, this man under the light of the porch, cigarette smoke like steam in the air, transistor sound of crickets in the woods. He's on the steps as you're out of the car—the lawn, the trees, everything underwater in the dark— and across the wet grass you're asking what you can do for him.

He's tall and ropy and down the front walk toward you, cigarette in his hand, you about to ask what's the problem when there's a click from the truck. It's only a door opening—but look how jumpy you are, how relieved to see only a boy in the driveway—the kid from this afternoon cutting straight to go to his father, the man tossing his cigarette into the grass, brushing his foot over it, apologizing for how late it must be.

How can I help you?

You're a police officer, says the man, aren't you?

And Sheila's out on the porch now—the light behind her—a silhouette at the rail, she's hugging a sweater around herself, her voice small like a girl's in the dark, asking if everything's all right, you taking a step toward the house and telling her that everything's fine, another step and you're saying you'll be right in, she should go back inside, it's late.

And once again, the man apologizes for the hour and says he'll only be a minute—your wife going into the house—this man on your lawn pulling the boy to his side, their faces shadowed and smudged in the dark, the man bending to say something to his son, the kid saying yessir, his father standing straight, saying that you helped put a dog down this afternoon.

And before you even open your mouth, he's stepping forward and thanking you for your help—the man shaking your hand, saying how pleased, how grateful, how proud, how difficult it must have been—but his tone's all wrong, all snaky, a salesman nudging his boy ahead to give you—and what's this?

Oh, he says, it's nothing, really.

But the boy's already handed it to you—the dog's collar in your hand, the leather almost warm, tags like coins—the guy's voice all silk and breeze as he explains how they wanted you to have it, a token of appreciation, in honor of all you did for them.

And it's a ship at sea to stand on that lawn like this—everything swaying and off-balanced for you—and before you say a word he's laughing as if to the trees, the man saying to put it on your mantle, maybe, or under your fucken pillow. Put it on your wife, he says and laughs and swings around all serious and quiet to you, the man saying he's sorry for saying that.

Nice lady, he says—the boy milk-blue in the night, cold and skinny as he stands next to his father—the man telling you how he made it home a little late after work that night. Was after nine by the time he and the kid got around to the dog, he says, dark when the two of them get out to the field—flashlight and shovel—almost decide to wait until morning.

Can't find her for the life of us, he says, but then we do—not like she's going anywhere—takes us a while to dig that hole, never seen so many stones, so many broken bottles.

He nudges the boy—startles the kid awake, it seems—and then turns to the house behind them, the yellow light of windows, the curtains, the blade of roofline, the black of trees, the shrubs. He lets out a long sigh and says it's a fine place you seem to have here. You say thanks—and then you wait—watch for him to move at you.

Any kids?

Two boys, you say.

Younger or older than this guy here?

Few years younger, you say.

He nods—has his hand on the boy's shoulder—you can see that much in the dark, can hear the sigh, the man deflating, his head tipping to one side slightly. So, he says, like I was saying, took us a while to get the hole dug. And when we go to take the collar, she tries to move away from us—still alive—all this time, she's been out there—imagine seeing how ants had gotten all into her.

He hums a breath and runs his palm over the boy's hair, says the vet arrives a little later, asks if we did this to the dog, makes us feel where you're supposed to shoot an animal, this slot just under the ear. He reaches his finger out to you and touches, briefly, the side of your head—almost tender—the smell of cigarettes on his hand, your feet wet and cold in the grass, jaw wired tight, the boy and his father letting you hang there in front of them, two of them just waiting for whatever it is you will say next to this, the man clucking his tongue, finally, saying, Anyway—helluva a thing to teach a kid, don't you think?

A pause—but not another word—and he starts them back toward the truck, the man and the boy, their trails across the silver wet of the lawn, the pickup doors clicking open and banging closed—one, and then another—the engine turning over, the headlights a long sweep as they ride away, the sound tapering to nothing. And in the silence, in the darkness, you stand like a thief on the lawn—stand watching this house for signs of life—wavering as you back gently away from the porch, away from the light of the windows, away until you're gone at the edge of the woods, a piece of dark within the dark, Sheila arriving to that front door, eventually, this woman calling for something to come in out of the night.

JEFFREY LEVINE

A Slight Illumination, a Pacific Vapor

Had he been able to sing... It was almost a song.
The phrases enveloped in his voice's flesh
Were of the hardness of a writing near at hand.
He would note: the kernel. The stone
On which he constructs a temple of music.
A school of gongs.

How to hold the earth in place.
Which accords us the grace to be what we can.
And before the traveling a "never"
That took the visible half of the world
From them, and in exchange, gave them the invisible.

Always the garden, but a lazy garden. Feckless.
Kept, the promise gave them bizarre riches.
Everything—
We could have had, we had.

The air where we meet, the beauty of the air where the street,
The café is found: a slight illumination.
A Pacific vapor.
Together in the interior where the impossible
Doesn't enter.

DAVID MASON

From the Anthology

Go tell the President: the wagon trail
was lost out there beyond the sinking sun.
The sun dance ended in a leaden hail.
The brooks have all forgotten how to run.

I found a feather but I lost the bird.
I sent out fifty scouts and they returned
with word that there would never be a word
for what the great society had learned.

I burned a library. I bombed a clinic.
I got myself embedded in a war
and slept and dreamed I was confirmed a cynic,
anointed with an oil worth fighting for.

I harpooned that imaginary whale
then made love to a reefer at the bar.
Go tell the President who made the sale
I don't think we have traveled very far.

The bridges crumble and the rivers rise.
A well-dressed man walks shouting down the street,
gesticulating toward the narrowing skies,
but what he says nobody can repeat.

The oracle has spoken. Simon says
your ears are burning and your eyes are red
so sleep it off on that decrepit *chaise*
then rise to meet the stranger in your bed.

This is the prophecy of Sunday night.
A working day will follow. Take a card.
You don't know who you are. You look a sight,
and yet you've been elected to the board.

Don't mention what you heard the salmon say.
Don't leave the evidence inside the case.
Don't flip a finger at our proud display.
Set all the tape recorders on erase.

Go tell your mother you were never born.
Go tell the keeper of the secret file
that every word contained there is forlorn
but every love you leave receives a smile.

This is the shopping list of your desire.
This is the bill that you can never pay.
Go tell the President. It's work-for-hire.
And pray you can remember how to pray.

MICHAEL MEYERHOFER

The Clay-Shaper's Husband

Here I am, confronting this bowl
kept under guard and pressurized glass
in the archway of the St. Louis Art Museum,
and somehow it feels good
to note that it's not all that impressive.

Clean, sure, and smooth, but plain.
Like this was just the demonstration piece
by the teacher of a pottery class
who has fired his kiln so many times
he could—and does—do it while drunk.

Then I see the note on the plaque
that says this was made by a woman,
which apparently they can tell
by the curves petrified within the swirl-print.
That, I decide, must explain the absence

of a hunt-carving. Say, a bison
turned sideways in an empty field
while some scrawny fool hefts a spear
that looks, coincidentally, about as thick
as his own and the bison's legs.

But this one lacks adornment,
which is a nice way of saying it's boring
to someone raised on video games,
who nods off in movie theaters
whenever spaceships stop exploding.

Now should be the story's turn
where I visualize the ancient woman
who shaped this and try
to pull off some simple, heroic ending
that shows her bronze wrists

deep in Nile mud, hair up, her infant crying
because that's what infants do
—especially in 2000 B.C.
without canned applesauce and Pedialyte.
I am leaving the museum now.

Giving up, I think not of my clay-shaper
but the men next to her. How one, at least,
must have thought it a miracle
when her small hands rounded the earth
and left it that way. How could he know better?

Perhaps this was the same man
whose eyes drew lines between the stars
while the others laughed at him.
No one saw the hunter, the bull, the ladle
no matter how he pointed.

But *she* saw, I bet. That's why
she gave him that bulb of pottery
the size of a baby cabbage.
Here, she said. *Love what you can touch.*
And he did, washing her small hands like jewels.

ROBERT MEZEY

Long Lines, Beginning with a Line Spoken in a Dream

The lines the dead man writes are like the lobster's skeleton
Through which the wind blows, picking its way along the rocky
   shore,
But make no sound. One hears only the grandeurs of the surf
And the froth sliding down the glassy sand. One learns to live
With this noise, which after all is beautiful and signifies
The promise of some meaning, some poetry
Of how life could be lived, and dreamed, and known—
Something beyond
These shells and boulders rotting in the sun.

The Other Tiger

> *And the craft that createth a semblance*
> —Morris, "Sigurd the Volsung" (1876)

I think about a tiger. Twilight exalts
The vast and never-resting library
And seems to make the shelves of books recede;
Powerful, innocent, new-made, stained with blood,
He will move through his rainforest and morning,
Will leave his spoor upon the muddy bank
Of a river whose name must be unknown to him.
(In his world there are neither names nor past
Nor future, only an eternal present.)
And he will cover inhuman distances
And sniff out in the winding labyrinth
Of odors the true odor of the dawn
And the delectable odor of a deer.
Among the bamboo's sunstripes I make out
The sway of *his* stripes and I have a sense
Of bone beneath the dazzle of rippling hide.
In vain the swelling seas, the mountain ranges,
The deserts of the planet come between us.
From this house in a somnolent, remote
South American port, I seek you, dreaming,
Oh tiger of the far banks of the Ganges.
Evening spreads in my soul and I reflect
That the apostrophized tiger of my poem
Is a tiger made of symbols and of shadows,
An endless string of literary tropes
And things remembered from encyclopedias,
And not the fatal tiger, the dread jewel
Who goes on under the sun or changeful moon
Completing in Sumatra or Bengal
His round of love and indolence and death.

Against this tiger of symbol I have opposed
The actual tiger, tiger of hot blood,

The one who decimates the buffalo tribe,
And today, 3 August 1959,
See, lengthening on the grassland afternoon,
A stationary shadow, but already
The fact of having given it a name
And dreaming up its habits and surroundings
Makes it a fiction, not a living creature
Among the living creatures of the earth.

It is a third tiger we are seeking.
Just like the others this will be a shape
Out of my dreams, a system of human words
And not the tiger himself, the vertebrate tiger
Who treads the earth, far beyond the reach
Of our mythologies. I know all this,
Yet something sends me on this open-ended
Ancient adventure, and I persevere
In hunting through the hours of afternoon
The other tiger, the one not in the poem.

after Borges

D. NURKSE

Altamira

We thought: after us
there will be a blue moth
flying jaggedly sideways.

Round dusty sparrows will peck
indignantly at the stone sill.

There will still be rolling clouds
and their shadows on Altamira
will fold in steep valleys.

After us, there may also be lovers,
stripping and trembling, bargaining
with the air between two bodies,
then fighting and reconciling
as if practicing an instrument.

But there will be no world.

Just you and I in the unmade bed,
bored and lazy, except it will be now
and only now, never again in memory.

Never again will it happen in words.

Bertrand de Born Smuggles a Letter Out of Hell

Dearest, I am happy in the fire.
The lighting is spectacular,
snaking tongues, a rain of sparks,
and the moans of the damned thrill me.

There is no death here. God's love
revives us at the brink of extinction.

The torments are cunningly varied
but there is not one that does not correspond
to a dream I wailed at as a child
before my mother heard and soothed me.

I was condemned for being the poet
who praises war, *trop estau en patz*.
So shadow destriers piss on me
and drag their shit-stained carapaisons
across my welts, and the infantry
who died at Beziers, young and callow,
pierce me with non-existent lances,

but suffering is just a story
I tell myself, as in the crib.
No fire can singe my mind
except our separation.

P.S. Dante passed here in a toga woven
of strangely fire-resistant merino
and I trusted him with this message.

I scored it on vellum with a live coal,
searing holes shaped like letters.

Darling, hold it to your hazel eyes,
and see my constancy, my will,
and through this play of gaps
see the world the living cannot notice
without a lens or a screen:

the oak forest, deep-shadowed in May,
our wedding village, white dressed stone,
Hautefort, the first defenses of Paradise.

ALICIA OSTRIKER

The Husband

When he is deep inside me suddenly I see
what he is doing: he is like a man in a tunnel

clay walls moist, tracks
gliding into the distance

he carries a weak flashlight
peers forward

What is he doing?
Is he afraid of snakes?

No, he is seeking the other man
the rival, the brother, the father

ALICIA OSTRIKER

Winter Trees

I am like the trees
not ruined exactly but shorn of ornament
and destitute of motivation

it is possible to find
both beauty and truth in their
pure forms

and I would like to do so
in myself if time could be persuaded
to hold off its heartless green

Agustín

The light in the morning made him happy. It was one of the few things that did now. It arrived discreetly filtered, not to disturb him, then poured in when Pablino came to open the shutters, lighting up the dark corners and bleaching the embroidery on the nineteenth-century bench at the foot of the bed. Agustín didn't care about the embroidery. His daughters did; they said it was fading. The bench had come from an estate auction, at which someone's children sold everything and split the money so they wouldn't fight. His daughters wouldn't have an auction when he died; they loved to fight, and would agree only in condemning his treatment of the furniture. When the generals were taking everything, all the best houses, Agustín had hidden his property behind unpruned trees, let the buildings go to hell, and drained the lake until it became a fetid swamp, something the generals could not want. When the junta was thrown out, and other families opened their houses for dances and dinners, Agustín didn't. He hired gardeners, and the lake filled itself back in, but he stayed alone, behind the trees. But today his daughter was coming to lunch. It was easier to hide from the generals than from those girls.

Alma, his elder daughter, was preoccupied with her spoiled teenage children, but found time to telephone him about nothing. Lucha, the younger, was very thin, and recently blond, and appeared in magazines with fruit on her head, which deeply upset her aunts. She was a singer, of sorts, and childless in her thirties. Agustín sometimes wondered if the girls would be more tolerable if their mother had lived. They had been thirteen and fifteen when she died of a virulent pneumonia—she had never been healthy—and it seemed to have arrested them at that selfish age.

Agustín read the newspaper in bed, finished the orange juice and croissant off the tray, and ate the remaining jam with the coffee spoon. Then he rose to go outside. He wanted to prepare an English lesson for Pablino, or to begin reading a new book that had arrived, about the battle of Trafalgar, but Lucha would interrupt anything he began.

He walked to the stables, where the groom had bandaged the leg of the new quarter horse. Agustín inspected the wrapping, to be sure it was clean, and the horse rubbed its heavy head against his shoulder, smelling of sweat and liniment. At the simplicity of the gesture, he felt a pang: the raw nerve of his loneliness exposed.

Out of loneliness, he had gone to a party in Buenos Aires for the Prince of Wales. He had watched the white-haired women in pearls and their men in dinner jackets, people who had railed against England over the Malvinas, shoving each other out of the way to get close to the prince. A woman had broken her necklace in the rush, and crawled after the pearls on the floor. Another had dug her heel into Agustín's shoe. They were hardy and ruthless, his contemporaries, these people who had survived everything.

It was that night after the party, as Pablino was driving him home on the bad roads, that Agustín had offered to teach the boy English. Pablino was an Indian, small and agile, with pockmarks beneath his high cheekbones. He was also an orphan, his father killed in the miserable war, his mother of an unnamed disease. Asked his age, he answered without confidence: he was twenty-eight or twenty-nine. He seemed both younger and older than his years. He wasn't forthcoming about his past, though Agustín knew he had picked cotton for his grandfather as a boy, and had rarely gone to school. He seemed uninterested in the future, although it was hard for Agustín to know. But he spoke of no plans.

"I must be too old to learn English," he said.

"Nonsense," Agustín said. "You're still a child."

They had begun with simple greetings the next day: good morning, hello, how are you. Pablino seemed politely interested in the lessons, but he gave nothing away, and Agustín thought he might seem politely interested if his employer offered to shoot an apple off his head.

Lucha and her husband arrived for lunch in their spotless gold car on the gravel drive. His skinny daughter climbed out in gold sandals that left her feet almost bare, and a buttery pantsuit that swung loose around her ankles. The husband had a gut like all Americans, and wore sunglasses and shorts. He spoke Spanish like a tourist, and made no effort to learn more. Agustín had a grudging respect for the man's stubbornness. They spoke English together.

"I have a new gun to show you," Agustín told him. "An elephant gun."

"Oh, those guns!" Lucha said. She kissed him on the cheek. "Why don't you ever come to the city, Papi? We miss you so."

He wasn't fooled by her flattery. He had been in an accident in a hired car not long ago, and Lucha hadn't been able to conceal her disappointment that he was still alive, spending her money. He tried to think back to a happier time—two round little girls in his lap, a living, loving wife—but it was no longer he. Children were experiments, and his had failed.

He led his guests to the patio for a drink. Lucha asked Pablino for a diet Coca-cola and his son-in-law asked for whiskey. Such things, before lunch.

"I wish you hadn't rented the summer house to the French lady," his daughter began.

"She's a good tenant."

"People take their lovers there, and pretend they don't have wives and husbands somewhere else."

"Oh, Lucha," he said. "What else is new?"

"They swim naked in the pool."

"And?"

"And it's embarrassing! Our caretakers are there."

"Adulterers tip well."

"Papi, don't you care about *anything*? If Mami were alive, she would care."

If Mami were alive. That was always the thing. "They are old bodies in an old pool," he said. "What does it matter?"

Lucha slumped back, pouting. "Well," she said. "You won't believe who came to me for a job. Inez Martín."

Agustín caught his breath at the rush of feeling in his chest. He shifted in his chair, trying to understand this news.

"Do you remember the Martíns?" Lucha asked. "They went away after Menem came. They lost everything."

"I thought she was in Italy."

"She came back," Lucha said. "She's been working here. I needed a second housekeeper, and Ofelia let her in and I saw her sitting on the sofa. I couldn't believe it. I used to idolize her. She was older than I was, and she was so glamorous, in beautiful clothes. And there she was, in a cotton dress and cheap shoes. She wasn't surprised to see me; she knew who the job was for."

Agustín waited for the rest of the story. The little black dog came to the table, the one the maid spoiled and the cook overfed, and Lucha began to rub its head. She made small kissing noises over the arm of her chair, and the dog wriggled with happiness.

"Her husband?" Agustín finally asked.

"He had a heart attack, I think," she said. "But he didn't die."

Agustín tried to remain composed. Inez Martín! She had utterly disrupted his life. They had met in the house of a friend, and she had talked very charmingly at dinner, and touched his arm in a way that gave him encouragement. It was a hundred years ago: twenty years ago, at least. She was much younger than he. He had persuaded her to meet him in the garden. Her dreadful husband was asleep in the house. Agustín's wife was dead, and Inez brought him back to the world. He remembered her warm breath and the taste of her, and the cold stone bench beneath them. He thought he had been saved. He had pursued her through other people's houses, meeting in empty rooms when the others were out. The chance of catching her eye and slipping away was what he lived for. He was exultant in the conquest. Then the inconvenient husband lost his position and his money, and Inez went with him to Italy, where he had family, to start again. The husband was a bore; not even failure could make him interesting. Agustín had begged her to stay, but she left, and he had heard nothing since.

"I couldn't hire her, of course," Lucha said. "She's my equal. I couldn't have her washing my underwear. So I sent her to the crazy French, who wouldn't know anything or care. Poor Inez."

"She's at the summer house?"

"I think so," Lucha said. "Imagine, with the naked guests!"

There was a long silence. The little dog yipped, at being ignored, and Lucha reached down to take its ears in both hands. "What *is* it?" she asked, as the dog panted with pleasure. "What is *wrong*, my love?"

"How about seeing that elephant gun?" the American husband asked.

"Such a waste of money," Lucha said.

"It's an investment," Agustín said, out of habit. "And I'm going to Africa."

Lucha looked up at him with her mother's big eyes. "What?" she asked.

The plan had not existed until that moment. He had killed a rhinoceros and a bear many years ago, and mounted them on the walls, but he was old now. Even the rhinoceros and the bear were shot under circumstances in which it was not difficult to shoot a large animal. He had bought the elephant gun because it was a magnificent firearm for his collection. But now he thought Africa might do him good.

"I'm going to kill an elephant," he said. He knew there was an English story about the embarrassment of doing so, but he couldn't remember it clearly. Why should he not shoot an elephant?

The three of them went to his office, where Pablino unlocked the glass case containing the best guns.

Lucha perched on the edge of the desk. "You're so lucky to have Pablino," she said in English. "Ofelia is hopeless. Inez at least would be smart. Someday I'm going to steal Pablino from you." She gave the boy a big, seductive smile.

Pablino passed the gun to Agustín, ignoring her. The boy might not understand her English, but he understood Lucha well enough. The gun was heavy, a six-bore rifle that could put a bullet through an elephant's skull. Agustín handed it to the American, who let out a low whistle.

"That's gotta have some kick," he said.

"I suppose so."

"Let's go see!" Lucha said, springing up off the desk.

Agustín had not thought of shooting the gun—the cartridges were expensive and the recoil was intimidating—but he felt himself pushed along by the children. Lucha had an idea where to go, and they all climbed into Agustín's little Renault, Lucha driving and Agustín in the passenger seat with the gun. The American folded his big legs into the back. They drove through the pastures, past the cows, and Agustín got out to open and close each gate. The sky was expansive and blue, and he found his own property majestic. He thought of Inez, who had never seen it—it was still an overgrown swamp when he was chasing her around other people's houses, keeping her a secret from his dictatorial teenage daughters. But she couldn't fail to find it majestic, too.

"Here," Lucha said finally, and she parked the Renault at the end of a road, by the lake that had been drained and now was full again. "We used to come here when we were little." She walked, looking up at the trees, her trouser legs swinging around her ankles. "There," she said, and she pointed. Above them, hanging like a giant wasps' nest from a high branch, was a brown woven bulb: a nest of papagayos.

"I'm not going to shoot parrots with an elephant gun," Agustín said.

"You should see if it works, before you go off to Africa." She was daring him, taunting.

"I want to go back to the house."

"Just try to hit *something*," Lucha said. She picked up a fallen branch with leaves still on it. "We'll put this on top of the fencepost, and you can shoot it off." She balanced it carefully across the post, brushed off her hands, and stepped back.

Agustín studied the branch on the fence, not twenty feet away. If this branch were the only kind of target he could hit, they would have to hold the elephant on a leash for him. He removed the safety, then raised the gun and fired. The kick was much greater than he expected, and he flinched. He missed the fencepost, but broke a piece of barbed wire that waved in the air. The parrots fled the nest overhead, screeching. He thought he might have dislocated his shoulder, the pain was so intense. He investigated the movement of the joint. The branch sat untouched, and the screaming of the birds faded into silence.

"You should be careful," Lucha said mildly, "that the elephant doesn't get angry and come after you."

"You want me to die anyway."

"Of course I don't!"

"I want to go back to the house." His shoulder was bruised and his hands trembled. He got in the car with the gun, and let the American open the first gate.

Riding past the field of alfalfa growing for winter hay, Agustín saw a hare out the window, darting along the road just ahead of them, and he knew he could shoot it. He would be ready for the kick now. He roared at Lucha to stop the car, and lifted the gun off his lap, keeping an eye on the hare. Then the car was filled with the loudest noise he had ever heard, as loud as a bomb, and the car shuddered as Lucha braked to a stop. A sharp smell of powder hung in the air. He looked down at the floor between his feet. A ragged circle the size of a dinner plate had been blasted away, and he could see the gravel of the road below. The engine still chugged.

Lucha swore loudly and shrilly. "What if that had been my *head*?" she cried.

It could more likely have been Agustin's own foot. He didn't look at her, or at her husband in the back seat. There would have been nothing left of the hare, in the unlikely event he had hit it. He kept his hands folded over the gun's hot chamber. Lucha stomped on the gas, and the car lurched forward. Agustín watched the hole in the floor, the road moving in streaks of gray and brown below. He was ashamed, but he wouldn't give his daughter any quarter. Lucha swore quietly to herself all the way home.

They drove along the windbreak of trees, past the lawn and up to the house. Pablino came out to meet them, looked alarmed, and helped him with something like tenderness into the house.

The three of them sat over an awkward lunch, Pablino bringing the plates and taking them away. The boy moved quietly and missed nothing. As the husband reached for a dropped fork, Pablino appeared with a new one on a plate. Agustín kept feeling the kick of the gun, and a ringing in his ears.

"Tell me more about the girl," he finally said, when the dessert came. "Inez Martín."

"She's not a girl anymore," Lucha said. "She's older than I am."

"How old?"

"Oh, God, maybe forty-five? She's not young."

It was hard to imagine. In his mind, Inez was in her twenties, a young wife, and he was trying to steal her away. At first, she said she couldn't leave her husband because she stood to lose everything. Later, she couldn't leave him because he had lost so much. And now she was working as a maid for a capricious Frenchwoman. Life could punch you in the throat no matter how you chose.

His daughter's husband stretched his arms, presenting his belly and big chest. "Want to go to the yacht club Saturday and look at boats?" he asked. "There's a race, so they'll have some good ones."

"I have to get the car fixed," Agustín said. "And make plans for Africa."

"Oh, Papi!" Lucha said. "*Africa.* You almost shot my head off!"

She gave Agustín a perfunctory kiss as they left. She smelled of flowers. He wondered how Inez smelled: of washing powder, or the kitchen, or some perfume from her life before. Lucha lifted her gold sandals delicately into her husband's car, and they drove away.

The Frenchwoman met Agustín at the door of his mother's house herself, not sending someone to do it. Her hair was chestnut brown and her face was stretched smooth, but he wasn't fooled. She was as old as he. She wore a long green silk robe with an embroidered neckline, and her arms were tan. He had called to say he would like to speak to Inez.

"It's wonderful to see you," the Frenchwoman said. "I've been so happy in your house."

He murmured some approving sounds.

"Inez is a good maid," she said. "Are you looking for someone to work? I can't spare her right away, but eventually I can, when I go to France. I can take with me only the ones I brought."

"Of course."

"There's a sitting room there," the Frenchwoman said. "You know the house, of course. Will you stay for lunch?"

"No, thank you," he said. "I'm engaged for lunch."

She shrugged in a French way, disbelieving him, still smiling. "I'll send her in."

The room was painted red. His mother had read to him there before dinner, when he was a child: a thrilling half hour of warmth and comfort, under a throw blanket, enveloped in his mother's perfume, with the dogs sitting at their feet. The walls had been pale yellow. There was a television in the corner now, and a wheeled liquor cart. He was still absorbing the changes when Inez Martín appeared in a pink maid's dress and a white apron. She wore her dark hair pulled back, and sat on the edge of a leather chair with her hands on her narrow knees. There were lines around the dark eyes he had loved, and the skin over her temples seemed very thin and pale, with a blue vein visible on one side, but she had the same pointed chin, the same clever mouth. His heart was racing. He hadn't expected to have all the old feelings in their full strength. He had thought they would be diminished by time.

"I thought you were in Italy," he said cautiously.

"I came back."

"And your husband? His heart?"

"He's recovering."

He nodded. She had a small, dark, triangular scar on her smooth bare shin. Her wedding band seemed loose on her finger. She had a slight accent, from the years in Italy. He tried to clear his mind. "You saw my daughter, Lucha," he said.

"I did."

"She's not my finest achievement."

Inez laughed. He remembered the way her laugh had charmed him that first night at dinner. "It was perverse to go to the interview," she said. "I was trying to destroy my pride, so it couldn't torment me anymore. The way they cauterize a wound. It didn't work. But it did get me a job."

"It's very good to see you."

"I don't know if it's good to see you. My old decadent life." She rested her elbow on the arm of the chair. "What news do you bring me? Is it as glamorous as I remember, or as sordid as it is here?"

"It isn't very glamorous."

"It's the most ugly thing you can imagine, here," she said. "People with everything, who take everything for granted."

"I'm sorry to hear that."

"Some are your friends."

"Once they were," he said. "I'm very much alone, these days."

She looked thoughtful. "Do you know what I miss?" she asked. "I miss orange juice in the morning, in bed. I miss someone bringing in a tray, and opening the windows."

Agustín felt an aching thrill at how easy this would be to supply.

"It's foolish, isn't it?" she asked.

Agustín said he didn't think it foolish at all. His heart felt dangerously full, for the first time in years. That dried up, battered organ, suddenly flush with love. It could kill him.

"It *is* foolish, though," she said. "The money is gone, and my husband thinks of nothing else. My son is in boarding school, so all the money goes there, and to the doctors."

He was trying to keep up. "You have a son?"

"Of course." She smiled and looked much younger, the way he remembered her. "He's thirteen," she said. "The age when they become awkward and skinny, but he is still so beautiful. The most beautiful child. All I want is for him not to be ashamed of me."

He wished he had known about the son. He had deliberately avoided gossip, but how had word of a child not reached him? Why had Lucha not told him?

"I would like you to marry me," he blurted. He hadn't intended to say it outright, but it seemed best to be direct, as she was. He had to lay his cards on the table.

"I'm married," she said, without surprise or resentment, after a pause.

"But are you happy? Does he treat you well?"

She studied his face. "You want to spite your daughters."

"No." He shook his head. He wanted to kiss her again in a dark garden, but the dream was complicated by the vision of a lanky adolescent sitting beside her in the shadows, glowering. "I could help your son," he said. "I could pay for the school."

"You weren't counting on a child when you came here."

"No."

"But you're serious."

"I always was." It wasn't entirely true. He had been too afraid of his teenage daughters to offer her marriage, then. He had been a fool.

She took another moment, as if thinking it through. "A déclassée housemaid leaving her child and sick husband for money," she said. "Imagine. Your servants would hate me, and your daughters would hate me, and my son would certainly hate me. I'm strong enough for this kind of work, but I'm not strong enough to be alone and hated."

Agustín took a moment to find his voice. He wanted to say that she wouldn't be alone, but he understood, with pain, that she didn't agree. "Where will you go when the Frenchwoman leaves?" he asked, through the haze of shame and disappointment.

"I'll find another job."

"You're not young." They were Lucha's words only, called up by his misery, because Inez did seem young to him.

She paused, and then she said, "No, I'm not. Is that what you came to tell me?"

"I only meant that the work must be difficult," he said. "You should have some relief."

"I know exactly how difficult my work is." Her voice was even, but not cold.

"I could help your son," he said, to keep her in the room. "Anonymously, for nothing. School fees, books, whatever he needs. Holidays. I would like to do that."

She laughed for a second time. "Lucha would love that."

"It isn't her money."

She considered him for a long moment. "It's tempting," she said. "But no, I think temptation is a dangerous thing. We have what we need. It's kind of you to offer."

"Please." He could hear the panic in his voice, at the thought of going home alone. He had refused to think that far ahead, to anticipate defeat, but now it loomed: the despair of the drive back, the months and years. "For your son," he said.

"It was kind of you to visit," she said. "I should help with the lunch." She rose, the woman he had wanted so desperately, and she smoothed the skirt of the pink maid's dress before she went out.

At the front door, the comically smooth-faced Frenchwoman touched his arm. She said, in a confidential tone, that Inez could act a bit *de haut*, but she was honest and did good work. If he wanted her sooner, that could be arranged. He should only let her know. Agustín could hardly reply, and couldn't hide his misery. Pablino opened the car door for him, with what seemed like an extra degree of care, and Agustín tried to control his trembling hands. If he held them tightly together, his hands were still, but then they were useless. The Frenchwoman watched them drive away. The little Renault had been deemed drivable, with a flat piece of wood covering the hole in the floor. He was going home to eat his lunch alone. He could go to Africa after all. He could let someone lead him to an infirm elephant and he could shoot it until it fell down. Pablino drove the damaged car carefully onto the paved road. It occurred to Agustín that the Frenchwoman's servants would have given Pablino a coffee while he waited, and the boy would have heard the gossip of the house.

"What do they say in the kitchen about the maid Inez?" he asked.

Pablino hesitated, and said nothing.
"You can tell me," he said.
"That she is beautiful."
"What else?"
"That she was rich once."
"They don't accept her."
"No."
Agustín nodded. So Inez was alone and hated already. She was living this way for her son, for whom she would do anything. He tried to imagine working as a servant in order not to make his daughters ashamed. It was ridiculous; the very act would shame them. There was a small, ugly part of him that wished for her son to recoil from her, because she had chosen servitude over his offer. But no, her son would love her, as he did. The boy made everything worthwhile for her. His existence made her grateful that Agustín had been too cowardly to defy his daughters for love.
"Is there anything this afternoon?" he asked Pablino.
"Nothing," Pablino said.
"Thank you for driving me."
Pablino glanced at him in surprise. It was his job. And it was awkward, Pablino's clear understanding that something significant had happened.
"I'm grateful," Agustín said stupidly. "You drive well."
The wounded car rattled along. He would go home and have his lunch, and Pablino would clear it away. They could have an English lesson; the boy would conjugate verbs if asked. There was the book on Trafalgar to begin. His older daughter would call to complain and brag about her children, to remind him that they existed, his heirs. Lucha would call to ask if the car was fixed and if he was really going to Africa.
He remembered the enormous sound of the gun going off in the passenger seat where he sat now, and he felt the kick again. A purplish bruise had developed on his shoulder. If Lucha had never come to lunch, he wouldn't have made a fool of himself in so many ways. He would never have fired the gun, or shot out the floor. He wouldn't have known that Inez Martín had resurfaced in his mother's house, and he wouldn't have presented himself to the vain, silly Frenchwoman, or prostrated himself before Inez. He would be living his muted and uneventful life, unbruised, with his

books and his horses and his house. If the trees could protect him from the pain that now gnawed at his heart, he would let them grow huge, but the trees could do nothing. He wanted to weep, but Pablino would be mortified, so he checked himself. He held his hands tightly together and cursed his daughter for bringing the terrible world, with its humiliation and longing, back to his door.

Tabasco in Space

I hear a generator buzz, I taste those days,
citronella swirled with cardboard meals
and ice unlimited, and the welcome thrill
of Katrina's king cake dolls, half-ounce bottles
of Tabasco packed with MREs marked
"Chicken Fajitas." People thought our food
was special made, a little heat singing
to the tongue of home, but I knew better.
Long have the McIlhenny's been men in arms,
and Tabasco has always traveled with them,
from saddlebags, to officers' tables,
to the final frontier—Tabasco in space,
floating from the dripper to the spaceman's lip.

What could be more American than
a Yankee banker ruined by the Civil War
come south to make it big with pepper sauce?

My worst job, worse than Taco Bell cashier,
was at Hill Memorial, a special collections library,
where it fell to me to tackle patrons fool enough
to sneak a pencil in the reading room.
Afternoons I worked behind the scenes
sorting donations, mostly major donor
McIlhenny stuff, his great-grands dumping crates
of a rich life's ticket stubs and corsages.

The librarians couldn't flat out refuse,
which meant shelf space dog-eared in the stacks
for resin hummingbird statuettes alongside
Audubon's *Wild Turkey,* collectible most high,
and print number one in *Birds of America.*
Protocol demanded white gloves, as on butlers of yore,

be worn when turning the folio pages
with tissue paper in between meant to keep
the reds from fading, red berries and beaks

living mostly in the archived dark.

They didn't end well, my library months.
I got so tired of filing letters to the world,
letters meant for home, the family bible's
apocrypha intercepted, transcribed, and shellacked.
Moss Madonna decoupage, and photographs
of slaves around the sugar pot, the children
battling stillness so hard that in the aftermath,
to history, they're just a blur.

I wonder
when they noticed my long, long lunch,
my blazer left behind on its peg, work
unfinished on the desk like an exhibit
at the Gallier House, all but the threshold
of the room roped off. If only I'd have thought
to tease them with a prank, something harmless,
like sharpening the golf pencils at both ends,
little footprints, Tabasco bottles placed
at random in the stacks—near Kingfish's
windbag letters, between gilt books in cages.
A fake collection, "The Hot Stuff Chronicles"—
among its contents a list of nonfood uses:
sentry-watch eye drops, cure-all for a sassy tongue.

Tabasco released a Charlie ration cookbook
as a joke, though I'd rather sample, say,
a Wisconsin marine's concoction,
the brain child of someone who eats cheese
on apple pie. Somebody sent me one
in a letter not long ago—did they jest,
or fear I'd turned survivalist after a peek
at my post-Katrina stash? So many ways
to spend a mouthful of vinegar and smoke.

Maybe I am crazy—awaiting the end of days
except for me and mine, who'll be hydrated and fed,
dressed in desert fatigues, and off the grid.

CATHERINE PIERCE

The Books Fill Her Apartment Like Birds

First just a few, then more, then more—
this one a gift, this one a pity adoption. They flutter
as she passes. They call
when she comes home. She strokes them,
soothes them. They flap, agitated.

She tries to nap, but their cries
are constant. They are starving.
They will not be placated. She says to her friends,
Look how they need me! She wraps herself
in their chattering demands.

They perch on her chest, her hands. Her bones
begin to decorate her skin. She eats
nothing now but what they feed her,
seed by seed. She thinks, *Now I am
beginning to exist.* Only at night

does she sometimes wish they'd quiet down.
Through the wall of sleep, she hears their shrieks
like pinpricks of light. In dreams, black lines of letters
drift into bars. She wakes
with her hands clenched like claws.

CATHERINE PIERCE

A Short Biography of the American People by City

In Surprise, every day is a party, streamers
in the trees and piñatas bursting. No one from Surprise

visits Dismal, though they've heard of its fog-
shrouded hills and barren streams. In Dismal they dream

of Happy and What Cheer, but it's all they can do
to someday make it to Boring, where homes are narrow

but clean and each dog is part Lab, part spaniel. The boys
in Boring long for the girls of Peculiar—they've heard

tales of leather and feathers, of lipstick the color
of tin cans and long hair the shade of the sky. The girls

of Peculiar are sick of the men from Ogle driving out
"just to visit." The girls are no fools. A camp counselor

once told them in hushed tones about her road trip
from Blueball to Intercourse to Climax, and since then

the girls have been wiser. Mothers want to pack them off
to Okay, where everyone's teeth are polished and all

boys under eighteen have cowlicks. When things go wrong
in Okay—the mayor's affair, the schoolteacher's lustiness—

the offenders start over in Nameless. The tired find strength
in Hot Coffee. The spiraling in Parachute. The hungry head

to Lame Deer, the clever to Riddle. A few men sneak off
in the night for Flasher and Footville, heads ducked

but thrilled to be fleeing Embarrass. And sooner or later,
when all their homes prove poorly named—when streamers

drop from trees, when cowlicks flatten, when poodles
start populating the parks—they all migrate east, crossing

rivers and hills to find one another in Fear Not.

RON RASH

Dylan Thomas

Scawmy, gray-souled November
blinds the whale-road, pall draper
over this ship bearing one
whose name means *of the ocean*
in a language he denied
allegiance to, though his lines
rang with cynghanedd—English
reined by Celtic music,
stitched tight as the coracle
that wombed Taliesin—tribal
rain-downs of sound, not enough:
a small people lose their tongue
one poet at a time. Talent-
squanderer, fraud, miscreant,
apt sobriquets for a life
lived badly between the lines.
The coast recedes. Last gulls cry.
Down in the hold his drunk wife
smokes and flirts with the seamen
who play cards on his coffin.

Shelton Laurel: 2006

Below this knoll a man kneels.
Face close to the earth, he works
soil like a potter works clay,
kneading and shaping until
hands slowly open, reveal
a single green stalk before
he palms himself up the row
as if he hauls on his back
morning's sun-sprawl, a bringer
of light he cannot bring here
where oak trees knit tight shadows
across the marble that marks
the grave of David Shelton.
Thirteen years old, he had asked
one mercy, not to be shot
like his father—in the face.
He shares this grave with the rest
killed with him that day, brought back
by kin so their bodies might
darken Shelton ground. Wind lifts
the leaves, grows still. A man sows
his field the old way. The land
unscrolls like a palimpsest.

JAY ROGOFF

Manhattan

You've got to have a little faith in people,
the girl says, blinking tears. She's seventeen,
the wise, shy center of a film where couple

after couple split, East Side lovers blown
round an unending storm, while past them whirl
parks, cafés, planetariums. The screen

(she's sobbing) swears by Woody Allen's smile
like lead anchoring a cathedral window.
It's Chaplin's awful grin to the blind girl,

joy raptured from our grasp, Gershwin's crescendo
opening our eyes to what we're really kissing.
Moral child, your course new-bent for England, you

ache with your old man's love-treachery, messing
up human fates on this small island. Granite
shifts underfoot, yet you tell this guy, piercing

your heart (again), *Have faith!* Faith! Who could want it,
some other silly girl, some other planet?
Oh brave new world that has such people in it.

CLARE ROSSINI

After a Woodcut of a Medieval Anatomy

Venice, 1448

Installed in a high wooden pulpit, the professor
Drones on aloud from his book, was it

Stephen of Antioch's spin on Abbas' translation of Galen the
 Greek?
The music of it all, anyway, the muscular rhythms,

Phrase knit to phrase with the delicate
Sinew of assonance—!

The students in the foreground milling about, pensive, drowsy,
 though
What's that fellow whispering to his mate?

Did you hear about Brabantino?
Got himself sloshed and screwed a prostitute with the clap.

No one looking at the body
But the barber, whistling as he draws his knife down the skin

Stretched tightly over the sternum, *Ecco*, then peels back the field
Of nipples and hair. No one looking, not for man to take in

The secrets of God, maker-in-chief—
The dead, God's dead, their bones, God's bones, God floating
 above them all,

Prone to anger, territorial, stalking the clouds of his
Hermetically-sealed heaven. And so ignorance perpetuated itself,

That's how we bright yearning moderns see it,
Who profess our love for the objective, who subscribe to
   unvarnished fact,

Though beyond the burbling fountains of this Venice.
Heaps of afterbirth in the muddy by-ways, shit steaming

Where it dropped from the beggar's leprous ass,
Even a doge stinking as he sits, palace-bound, in his silk skivvies,
   decaying

From the feet up. No wonder the mind
Sought its renaissance swagger, gravity postulated, gravity
   ascertained,

The lithe figures of calculus set down, the gaze
Sent gallivanting among stars...

A century after wood was scored to hold this scene, Vesalius
Will grab the knife from a gaping barber

And cut deftly into the cadaver's gray face, roaring to his students
Galen the Greek, the renowned and magnificent,

Riddled with error, gentlemen, look:
The jawbone's not one piece but two.

Was that the crowning moment of all
That we, earth creatures, can be?

Or just before, when we sat
In gloomy light, the fact of death before us as we gossiped or
   yawned

Or listened to the books of the ancients, who got it all wrong
Beautifully?

FAITH SHEARIN

Each Apple

At thirty-nine each apple reminds
me of some other. The memory lives
in objects: fallen from trees or baked
like pie. I kiss my daughter and
remember my own face kissed.
All Broadway music is from a play
I saw with my father when his
eyes were fine. Certain words
or smells evoke the faces of people
who have disappeared like mice.
Every taste or emotion is complicated
by the tastes and emotions of another
time. Perhaps this explains why
the very old don't leave their houses,
why they eat no more than a few bites?
Drunk, full really, on memory
there is little room for anything new.
Each word has been spoken by a
thousand voices, each face is another
face rearranged. Night grows
thin and sticky as a spider's web:
even blue moons are not so rare.

Trees

They know how to stay in one place.
Each year a circle: no need for photos
or taxes. They are dressed for the weather,
never stuck inside on a lively day.
Tongues of green light: their voices
made of wind. To climb one is
to leave the peopled world behind.
They cast such shadows: big lizards
in a city of buildings, alive
with all the birds cannot contain.

MAURYA SIMON

St. Jerome the Hermit

The chilly blood stands still around my heart.
—Virgil

Self-banished to the Chalcis desert for three years,
Hieronymus delved deeply into his sacred texts,

sleeping little and eating less, lingering for hours
in the hush of dawn to recite a litany of vows,

to compose copious epistles to church elders,
and to purify his sunburned body until it shone

as a fitting, sacred temple for the Holy Spirit.
A student of Hebrew, Greek, Latin, Aramaic,

he became a bastion of knowledge, a stronghold
of biblical lore, his memory dazzling, his vast

commentary acute, but troubling to some of
his fellow clerics, whose messages from Rome

urged him to purge himself of so much learning,
idolatry of the intellect, too stringent an asceticism.

Sometimes he wearied of words. Sometimes
the world beckoned in wanton ways: summer's

exuberance warbled and trilled outside his door;
then lewd thoughts would singe his aims, encoiling

him in unchaste shows of yearning, his blood
scalding his veins, his body rigid and pulsing.

There were days of blowzy light, when he flinched
to hear the sultry voices of distant washerwomen;

when even the sound of burbling water stirred him,
or the sight of an earthworm's swollen clitellum—

when the deft, rhapsodic mating of damselflies
wholly undid him, brought him to a misery of

fidgeting, so that he had to plunge his hands into
brambles to punish them for kneading his groin.

Even his dreams tormented him with impure visions
of Ruth or Sarah, of Bathsheba purloining David's gaze

as she bathed, of the slow unveiling of her limbs,
the sleek anointing of her breasts, thighs, lips.

Spasms of anger seized him on waking, driving him
to orgies of prayer, or to shatter another wasp's nest

under his roof, so his face and arms would bear,
unshielded, the barbed attacks of swarming daggers.

But he grew stronger. He outmatched his longings
for flesh with his striving toward redemption—

remedying himself with a remoteness toward others,
housing himself in sanctity like a priest's reliquary,

where he could polish the sacred bones of his belief
into a wintry splendor, a brittleness beyond touch.

(Chalcis Desert, 375 C.E.)

GERALD SHAPIRO

Mandelbaum, the Criminal

In a hospital in Kansas City, Stan Wachtel's wife, Celia, was dying. Outside it was the middle of February, raw and blustery, but in her hospital room the air was thick and warm, perhaps heated by the glow of all the machines monitoring her bodily functions. Her heart, that wretched fist, pumped listlessly, as if it had better things to do. Her doctors made a big show of shrugging and throwing their hands in the air. *Que sera, sera*—that was their theme song. None of their unpronounceable procedures, their mysterious protocols, the array of pills and fluids they pushed down her throat and dripped into her veins seemed to do Celia any good at all. Modern technology: a nightmare. Wachtel had long ago turned his back on the amazing march of progress; anything more complicated than a toaster made him queasy. He could grasp the purpose of a toaster: you put in bread, it came out toast. All the rest of it, the pint-sized gadgets of the computer age, seemed to him like so much crap: the promise of ease, of recovery, of everlasting life, and it was all worth nothing. These quacks might as well have put leeches on her back, sacrificed a cat at the foot of her bed.

Wachtel stared at the television bolted to the wall of her room. On CNN the pope—not the new one, whatever his name was, the old one, the polack, the cherubic polack who played the guitar—was washing the feet of the Turkish bastard who'd tried to kill him so many years ago. The sound was muted, so Wachtel didn't know what was going on. Maybe this was the anniversary of the old pope's death, or the anniversary of the attempted assassination. Who keeps track of such things? It was a nice gesture, washing the feet of the jerk who pumped a dozen bullets into you, but the pope, the poor guy, was a total mess, crippled up by Parkinson's Disease; he could hardly get down on his knees so he could wash this fanatic's feet; he had to be helped by his aides, and how the hell were they going to get him back up on his feet when he was done? They'd need heavy equipment to lift the guy. He'd be dead weight. Wachtel tried to imagine their rabbi, Silberberg, now a senile wreck, trying to wash anyone's feet. Silberberg, still handsome at eighty-two and natty in his Italian suit, had been by to see Celia twice so far. The second time he'd come, he'd forgotten her name in the middle of the visit. He seemed bewildered, as if he didn't know where he was.

Every fifteen minutes the cuff on Celia's arm automatically registered her disastrously high blood pressure, and the dismal results were flashed to the nurses' station down the hall. Doctors arrived in swarms once or twice a day on their rounds, crowding the room, accompanied by a roving gang of bleary-eyed medical students, most of them so young they might have been teenagers dressed in doctor's outfits. They flipped through her charts, these overgrown children, they made clucking noises, thumbed through soiled reference manuals, played with their stethoscopes, whispered furtively in the far corner of her hospital room.

Once he grabbed the lapel of one of the older doctors and managed to establish eye contact. "Stan, what can I tell you?" the fellow said. "Things aren't looking all that good." He was a small man, bald and hump-backed, with a long, pink-tipped, aquiline nose. He wore an inappropriately festive floral bowtie. "I'm sorry," he said. "She's just old. Her heart's tired."

This was hardly news to Wachtel. The woman was eighty-five years old, and they hadn't been easy years. Long ago, another lifetime it often seemed, a son, Arnold, their only child, a boy of enormous promise, had been the joy of their existence. He'd risen through life like a shooting star: valedictorian of his high school class, scholarships to Berkeley, a Ph.D. from Michigan in Anthropology and Psychology; his first book (published when he was all of twenty-six), *The Sneering Chimp: Facial Expressions and What They Tell Us*, won a major prize, ensuring his tenure at Princeton. He was interviewed repeatedly on PBS; his views on contemporary culture were often quoted in *Newsweek;* a new adjective entered the world of current psycho-anthropological theory: *Wachtelian*. The pride his parents had felt! The sheer bursting joy of simply being able to claim him as their own! But then tragedy beat the life out of them: on a research trip to the jungle of Belize, exploring the varieties of laughter among a remote, previously undocumented tribe, Arnold had wandered away from his colleagues one morning and was never seen again. For years Celia had waited by the phone; she'd broken her heart over this lost boy, had wept over him until there were no more tears left to cry. What was there to say about such a life? Her parents, immigrants who'd never learned English, were of course long dead. She was estranged from her fractious, undistinguished siblings back East; her working years had been spent in a series of lackluster clerical positions; she'd lost her looks long ago. Now, seemingly oblivious to the daily parade of doctors and nurses, she lay quietly in her hospital bed, her shins wrapped in inflatable plastic leggings to keep the swelling at bay. February lurched by a day at a time, each moment more dreadful than the last; she shrank into herself, retreating closer and closer to death. To keep her edema in check, her doctors cut off her fluid intake, and Wachtel, sitting at her bedside, mute with grief, swabbed her cracked lips with a tiny sponge soaked in water. She'd had a small stroke shortly after arriving at the hospital (she'd choked momentarily on a bit of food, a nurse told him; that's all it took), and one half of her face had fallen, so her expression seemed perpetually ironic. What would Arnie have made of this? How did his study of facial expressions cope with the disfigurement of stroke victims? She'd never been an ironic woman, so this was something new. Wachtel looked at her. Was this his wife? Was this Celia?

"Maybe a week," the bowtied doctor told him one morning. Wachtel had been reading his *Kansas City Star*, and put it down in his lap, folded it into thirds.

"A week?" he asked softly.

"It's a guess. Don't quote me, Stan. I don't know."

Late that afternoon an elderly pear-shaped man shuffled into the room and sat down heavily in a chair by Celia's bed. The chair sighed as air leaked out of the cushions. He wore a pale blue windbreaker, white slacks, and gray orthopedic walking shoes with velcro snaps at the instep. His face, dominated by enormous sunglasses, was cast into a puffy, mournful sack; his mouth hung open as if he might be expecting a spoonful of pudding. After a moment he took off his glasses, put his head in his hands and began to weep. He shuddered and wailed, beat his fat fists against his temples. This all happened so suddenly that Wachtel didn't even have time to say hello. He sat frozen in the lounge chair by the window. Though Celia had been in the hospital for ten days already, she hadn't had many visitors besides dotty old Rabbi Silberberg—most of their friends, the doddering couples they sat with at *shul*, their bridge partners, Wachtel's old business associates, were in Florida or Arizona this time of year—and now this, out of the blue, a total stranger comes into the room and has a nervous breakdown. From across the room he could smell the man's cologne.

The wailing tapered off at last, and the visitor straightened up in his chair. He put his sunglasses on again and looked around the room. "Oh," he said when he saw Wachtel by the window. "It's you. Stanley, am I correct?"

Wachtel was taken aback. "Excuse me? Do we know each other?"

The visitor's plump fingers were festooned with costume jewelry, the stones looking like something he might have gotten from a box of Cracker Jacks. He twisted one of the rings now, rotating it as though trying to unscrew his finger from his hand. "I'm Cheeky. Celia's brother."

Wachtel couldn't believe it. But of course, yes, he saw the resemblance. The nose, the predatory cast of the lips, the chin. "No," he said, but he knew it was true.

"It's me."

This Cheeky Mandelbaum was a legend in their family. He'd gone to prison (Attica, Sing Sing, Wachtel couldn't remember which one, or maybe it was both) in the long-ago past. Celia never mentioned the crime, and Wachtel, too timid to probe into something so painful, had never asked. Something white-collar, he imagined—embezzlement, check-kiting, mail fraud. A Jew wouldn't have got involved in anything violent. But then he thought of Meyer Lansky, Longy Zwillman, Bugsy Siegel: murderers, all of them. Well, who knew? They were desperate times back then, the Lower East Side was a fetid slum, the most overcrowded square mile on earth; people who wouldn't have turned to crime under normal circumstances did what they could to get ahead or stay afloat. He'd heard the story again and again, how Celia's saintly mother had died in the kitchen of their tenement flat, clutching the telegram that had brought her the news of Cheeky's conviction. "Hersheleh! *Gevalt!*" she moaned, and slumped to the floor, felled by a massive heart attack. Celia had told him this story so often that he could see the scene played out inside his head, could hear the thump of the woman's body hitting the cheap linoleum. This Cheeky, this *mamzer*, this nothing. Now here he was, the bastard, sitting across the room. What a pathetic piece of garbage. He didn't look like an ex-con. He looked like a retired insurance salesman down on his luck. *This* was Cheeky Mandelbaum, the criminal?

"What are you doing here?" Wachtel said.

"My sister's dying, ain't she?" Cheeky kept his head down; he seemed to be gazing at the velcro snaps on his shoes.

"So how'd you hear about it?" asked Wachtel. "Where'd you come from? The moon?"

"They said a *Mi Sheberakh* for her in *shul* yesterday."

"You go to *shul*?"

"Teferith Israel. Out on Metcalf."

"You live here? In Kansas City?" Wachtel felt his blood pressure taking off like a bottle rocket. "How could you live here?"

"For forty years. You don't remember running into me at the Brooklyn Deli on Troost?"

"So that was you!"

Wachtel remembered the scene vividly. A Sunday morning, early, he and Celia were there to buy lox, smoked sable, some whitefish salad, a few bagels, some cream cheese. It was an extravagance, but they only did it once or twice a month, and what other pleasures did they give themselves? This would have been around the time their son, Arnold, was starting to rise into the stratosphere. Three, four nights a week Arnold got calls from college recruiters pitching their wares. Amherst one night, the University of Chicago the next, dangling full scholarships, stipends to cover research and travel, winter tri-mesters in the Loire Valley, summer programs trekking through the Himalayas. Arnie had started smoking cigarettes at night in his room, had raided the small cache of alcohol in the sideboard in the diningroom. He'd been watering the bourbon, sneaking a shot now and then, and the truth was, who could tell him to knock it off? Every time Wachtel tried to speak to the boy he felt his tongue cleave to the roof of his mouth. His business was going down the tubes, there were arguments, recriminations, evenings spent in silence. Now Celia tugged at his sleeve as they stood in the Brooklyn Deli waiting for their number to be called by one of the tattooed workers behind the counter, Holocaust survivors, all of them, the women with their hair dyed garish shades of red, the men sallow, yellow-toothed, their haunted eyes rimmed by dark circles.

"What?" Wachtel said to her. "What is it?" They'd argued that morning in bed, something about the house, the gutters, money for this or that, he couldn't remember, he'd been half asleep; but all their arguments, no matter what the subject, were arguments about Arnold, what college would be best for him, what trajectory his brilliance might mark in the night sky.

"Over there," she whispered in his ear. "By the pickles." He turned his head. "Don't look!" she hissed. "Don't look. Just listen to me. That's my brother."

"Your brother," he echoed, his tone cynical. Celia had three brothers: Moe, a dimwit who ran a sandwich stand near Times Square; Julius, a Flatbush costume jewelry salesman with an eye for the ladies; and Cheeky, the brilliant eldest son, the one with all the promise, the black sheep of the family, who'd gone to prison.

"Cheeky," she whispered. "It's him. I swear to God it's him. I haven't seen him in twenty-two years, but it's him."

"What are you talking about? How could your brother Cheeky be standing there by the pickles? This is Kansas City, for crying out loud; he's in prison in New York State."

"He got out."

Wachtel looked at the numbered slip of paper in his hand. "You're telling me that's your brother Cheeky over by the pickles."

"Go over there, Stanley, and talk to him," she said.

"Celia. Why would I do that?"

She tugged on his sleeve again. "Go over there." Tears welled in her eyes.

He handed her the numbered slip. "Remember, poppy seed bagels, not the sesame. And the scallion cream cheese. And don't forget the sable, the lox. We'll have a spread."

"Just go over there."

"Smoked whitefish salad. And some halvah. Just a little piece. And get a loaf of the seeded rye. And some pastrami, half a pound, tell them not too lean for a change."

"Ask him if he's my brother. He owes me ten dollars. It was all the money I had in the world, I gave it to him and he disappeared. I want my money back."

"And if you get pickles, get the half-sour. I like the half-sour." He was about to add to the list, but he saw that she was crying now, so he squeezed her arm and walked over to the man by the pickles. He was an ordinary looking guy, round-shouldered, slack-jawed, a little broad in the beam—Jewish of course, as was everyone else in the deli on this Sunday morning. He wore a Lacoste shirt and a pair of Bermuda shorts, though the temperature outside was brisk. A pair of sunglasses rode atop his balding head.

"Excuse me," Wachtel said when he reached the pickle barrel. "My wife over there—" he pointed over his shoulder—"thinks you're her brother. Celia. Celia Mandelbaum, that was her maiden name. Stanton Street, Lower East Side."

The man stared at him impassively for a long moment in silence. "I don't have any family," he said.

Wachtel waited a beat, expecting the man to add something to his pronouncement, but when nothing more was forthcoming he shrugged and returned to Celia, squeezed her shoulder, then took the numbered slip back from her just as their number was called. At home he laid out the spread, the smoked fish, the bagels, the cream cheese, all of it, but she refused to eat. She went into the bedroom and shut the door and didn't come out until evening. It was a full day before she asked him what the man by the pickle barrel had said.

That was forty years ago, and now across the room from him sat Cheeky Mandelbaum in the flesh. It was like being in the same room with Frank Sinatra, Wachtel told himself, then shook off the thought. No, it wasn't like being in the same room with Frank Sinatra. It was like being in the same room with a 160-pound pile of garbage. "You broke your sister's heart," Wachtel told him. "You killed your own mother."

"People die. Don't put that off on me. My mother was a heart attack waiting to happen."

"What are you doing here?"

"You know what she ate for dinner most nights, my mother? A slice of rye bread rubbed with garlic then smeared with chicken fat, a little salt, with a slice of onion on top. That was what killed her. Chicken fat. Schmaltz."

"She was poor. It wasn't her fault."

"She was a good woman. Bessie the Good, that's what they called her around the neighborhood. I loved her, everybody loved her. She wasn't the sharpest knife in the drawer, but she had a heart of gold. Any *shnorrer* who knocked on the door, she gave him a potato. But she didn't care take of herself. So what happened, happened."

"She was poor!"

"You think that woman ever ate an orange in her life? She must have weighed two hundred pounds, she wasn't even five feet tall. What I'm saying is, what I'm telling you, she didn't take care of herself."

"Lots of poor people are fat."

An awkward moment of silence ensued. The two men stared at each other balefully. At last Cheeky sighed, exhausted, as if pushing a raft of memories out to sea. He nodded toward Celia, who lay semi-comatose in her bed. "What's the word on my sister?" he asked.

"Nothing. A week, maybe."

"She's dying? That's what they're telling you?"

"They can't do anything for her," Wachtel said with a shrug. "Her heart's giving out."

Celia moaned softly in her bed. Wachtel swabbed her lips with the moist sponge.

"You'd think they'd let her have a drink of water," said Cheeky.

"She had a stroke. She can't swallow anything. She'd choke. It'd go right to her lungs, she'd be dead."

"You said yourself she's dying, Stan. What's the difference?"

"Dying ain't the same as dead," Wachtel said, and rolled the sponge from one side of Celia's lips to the other.

In the cafeteria downstairs, rows of gigantic hearts made of construction paper hung from the ceiling, with "HAPPY VALENTINE'S DAY!" in bright, sequined letters painted on each one. Valentine's Day? Wachtel hadn't even thought about its impending arrival. Who thought about such things when a wife was in the hospital? He bought two cups of tea and a cheese danish for the two of them. He pushed Cheeky's tea to his side of the table, then cut the pastry neatly in half. Valentine's Day. He thought of elementary school, the foolishness of Valentine's Day, Arnie coming home so happy because the Blumkin girl had given him a Valentine's Day card with her lipstick on it, a seven-year-old girl, mind you, wearing lipstick and planting a kiss on a piece of paper. He sipped his tea. Around them, morbidly obese nurses moved in bovine, placid herds, carrying trays loaded with the detritus of their meals. Wachtel stared at them. How could people in the health care industry let themselves go like that?

"At least now she's in a private room," he said to Cheeky. "The first week, she was in a double, with a woman dying of colon cancer. Poor woman was so doped up she didn't know what county she was in. Her children sat there crying. That was no day at the beach."

"I knew a guy once," Cheeky began, and took a tentative sip of his tea. "He told me he was sitting on a toilet, on a train. I don't know when this would have been. Fifteen years ago, twenty maybe. Doesn't matter. Anyway, he flushes the toilet while he's still sitting on it, and the suction of the flush, it sucks his colon—his colon!—right out of his body. You believe that?"

"That's disgusting."

"He had to wear a bag. You know."

"That's impossible. It's ridiculous."

"I'm just saying this is what the guy told me." Cheeky sipped his tea delicately, one pinky extended. "He sued Amtrak, won a bundle." He ate a small bite of his half of the cheese danish, then pushed the rest of the piece into his mouth and swallowed it without chewing.

"Why would you even repeat a story like that?" said Wachtel.

Cheeky shrugged. "It's called making conversation." He paused, took another sip of his tea. "This is cold," he said, and moved the tea cup away with the back of his hand. "My father loved tea. He used to drink his tea out of a glass. He'd put a cube of sugar in his mouth, he'd hold it there between his teeth and sip the tea through it. Like they did in the old country."

"I've heard many stories about your father."

"He was a nothing," Cheeky said. "The man had the imagination of a doorknob."

"Celia adored him. She'd start to talk about her father, tears would come to her eyes."

"His favorite word was no. He got this from God, he told me. Saying no was his way of imitating The Almighty. He never had an original thought in his entire life."

Now it was Wachtel's turn to shrug. "So what. You didn't get along. It happens. Fathers and sons."

"This was different, Stan. Take my word for it."

"You were a bum," said Wachtel. He leaned closer over the table. "What are you doing here? What'd you come for?"

"I can't come see my baby sister, she's on her deathbed?"

"You had forty years to come see us, you never darkened our door."

"I didn't think she'd want to see me."

"She didn't!"

Cheeky spread his arms in a gesture of surrender. "That's what I'm saying."

"Why should she want to see you? You left her and the rest of the family high and dry. You were the one with all the promise! You were the genius! Some genius. Look at you!"

"I didn't turn out so bad."

"You borrowed ten bucks from her, she told me all about it, I know what I'm talking about. This was 1930, it was all the money she had in the world, she gave it to you, her older brother Cheeky, wonderful brilliant Cheeky, Mr. Charming, with the flower in his lapel."

"I don't recall."

"Don't give me that line. You know what ten bucks was back then?"

"I'm telling you the truth, I don't remember what you're talking about."

"She was saving that money. You told her you'd pay her back the next week. What'd you do with it?"

"How would I know? It was a long time ago. Bet it on a pony, maybe."

"Her father told her not to do it."

"That was Pop. Whatever the question was, his answer was no."

"So she disobeyed him, she did it anyway and what did you do? You flew the coop."

"I was young, I made mistakes. You're lucky, you never made a mistake in your life." Cheeky examined his fingernails and buffed them on his sleeve.

Wachtel fell silent. His mistakes crowded the room; they took up all the oxygen; they yammered in his ears like a pack of hyenas. At home there was a closet stuffed with twenty-five thousand feet of moldering Super-8 film stock, so many reels of it he'd never bothered to count them. This was one of his biggest mistakes: getting into the tourist souvenir film business just as videotape cameras were making their way into the marketplace. Videotape! The bane of his existence. His life savings were in that closet, all that film turning to toxic sludge in those canisters, each one the size of a can of tuna. He still remembered Greenstein, the bastard who sold him the business, the line of crap he'd bought from this old *joskie*, the handshakes, the assurances, the absolute iron-clad money-back guarantees that had been mentioned in passing, but somehow never made it into the multi-paged contracts that Wachtel had signed. Greenstein sauntered off into retirement, his bald head buffed to a high sheen, having divested himself of his entire stock of Super-8 film, camera equipment, developing chemicals, the whole shmear, just in time. For Wachtel there was nothing to do but watch as tourists, yokels from noplace, disembarked from the giant paddle-wheel steamers at Kansas City's riverfront, whole gangs of them, videotaping themselves as if they'd been doing it all their lives, mugging for their tiny cameras, singing and whooping, their appetites up for barbecue and shopping on the Country Club Plaza. They passed by Wachtel's little stand ("Take Home a Souvenir Film of Yourself in Kansas City! $10 For Five Minutes of film! Developed and Shipped to Your Home Address!") without even giving it a glance—he might as well have been invisible—and within a year, he'd lost everything.

"So what are you here for, really?" he asked Cheeky. "You borrowed ten bucks in 1930, now you're coming back for more?"

"What do I look like, a panhandler? Of course not. What are you talking about?"

"We don't have a dime. You say you've been living in Kansas City forty years—"

"Off and on. Not the whole time. I traveled. I went places you've never heard of."

"—it never occurred to you to stop by and say hello? So what are you showing up now for? You think you're in her will? What will? Forget about it. She doesn't have anything."

"I'm not asking for anything. I'm a retired businessman. I don't need anybody's money. I have investments. Half the checks I get in the mail, I don't even cash them, they sit in a drawer." Cheeky brushed crumbs off his shirt. "You think this was easy for me? Coming here like this, after all these years? I was so scared, I stopped in the toilet down the hallway before I went to Celia's room, they had one of those electric eye urinals? You make a move the thing flushes on you? I had the shakes so bad, it flushed five times before I could get my fly unzipped. I don't like that electric eye. The thing's looking at you while you're taking a leak."

"It's not looking at you."

"Why do they call it an electric eye, then?"

When they returned to Celia's room—they'd been gone no more than half an hour—she was dead. She lay in her bed in exactly the same position she'd been in when they'd left; a casual observer wouldn't have seen a bit of difference, but Wachtel knew immediately that she was gone; the body of an old woman was still beneath the covers, but Celia had flown away. He hovered by her bed for a long moment, waiting to see her chest rise, and then waited another long moment, and then another. He touched her skin, which had turned a pale yellow, like the color of milk gone bad. Her cheek was cold. He went to the door and shouted, "Nurse!" and in a moment a pair of nurses came bustling in to confirm the news. One of them scribbled information onto a form while the other lifted Celia's wrists one by one, then moved her head back and forth and opened and closed her eyes. It was all over very quickly. After so many desperate days of watching her slip away an inch at a time, Wachtel now wanted nothing more than to sit back and watch her slip away a bit more, just one more day of watching her die; he would have given anything to have the chance.

An hour later, he'd signed all the forms. Cheeky sat slumped in a chair by the door, his eyes half-closed. Wachtel stared at him: was the man napping? Catching a few winks in the aftermath of his sister's death? There was no bottom to this man. There was no decency. He walked down the hall to the nurses' station and said his goodbyes. He'd come to know some of them, the more garrulous ones with stories to tell. They squeezed his hand now, patted his shoulder, murmured unintelligible phrases of regret, but it was all gibberish to him. They might as well have been speaking in tongues.

Wachtel gathered Celia's personal items from the shallow closet in her room. He stuffed her shoes, her stockings, her underwear, her dress into a plastic bag, then dropped her purse in, too. He thought of her the summer they met, the dress she was wearing the night they'd danced together at the Tip Top Tap on Michigan Avenue in Chicago, two weeks before he shipped out. Dukey Willingham's Orchestra played. It was hot up there, steamy, something wrong with the ventilation, too many people and not enough air. That dress was something. Blue, something silky, not silk, though. Silk was going into parachutes at the time. It didn't amount to much, that dress. It must have weighed two ounces. She was small, slim, very young, she wore her hair like the Andrews Sisters, he could feel her heart pounding when they danced.

He kicked Cheeky in the ankle. "Hey. Wake up. It's over."

"What?"

"She's dead. Your sister's dead. Celia. She passed away."

Cheeky ran a hand roughly over his face. "That's impossible. My baby sister?"

"Don't start with that."

"My baby sister? Dead?" Cheeky lurched out of his chair. He could move quickly for an old man. He must have learned that in prison, Wachtel told himself. Knife fights in the exercise yard and all the rest of it. You had to be fast on your feet.

"C'mon," he said, and pulled at Cheeky's elbow. "It's over. We gotta go now. They need the room."

Downstairs in the lobby he didn't know what to say. "You need a ride?" he asked.

"I'm not going anywhere in particular," Cheeky muttered.

Wachtel looked at him, one eyebrow arched.

"I don't have anywhere to go," said Cheeky. He ran his tongue over his lower lip. "I'm between places right now."

"What's that supposed to mean?"

Cheeky regarded him silently for a long moment. "I had a couple of setbacks lately. Minor setbacks, temporary, Stan. I'll get back on my feet."

"You're broke, aren't you. That's why you showed up here. Celia was right. You're nothing but a thief. You're a criminal. You were a criminal when you were a kid, you're a criminal now. What's wrong with you? Do you have some sort of screw loose in your head?"

A middle-aged couple passed them, and as they went by, the woman clutched her purse to her bosom tightly, as if afraid of being mugged. Wachtel noted this and realized that he and Cheeky were making a scene here in the hospital. He'd lived his whole life trying to be decent, trying to keep his head above water and his picture out of the newspaper, and look how things had turned out. He'd wanted to own a small business, employ a few people, meet a payroll, pay his bills, prosper, leave something behind. After the tourist Super-8 fiasco he'd worked a series of dead-end retail jobs for years, selling crap, hating his bosses, saving every extra penny. Arnie was already gone by this time, his brilliant star having risen and exploded. His name was still mentioned now and then in journals of Psychology and Anthropology, but not often. Friends at *shul* asked questions occasionally. Any word? Of course there was no word. Eaten, by piranhas or leopards or cannibals, felled by mosquitoes, a poison dart, dysentery. Who knew? Arnie was a memory, a brief montage of scenes, snippets of dialogue. Wachtel couldn't remember his son's voice anymore. In the house, Arnie's ghost was faint, just a certain cast of light and shadow that played in the corner of his peripheral vision.

Wachtel was well into his seventies at the time, too old for new business ventures, but he was desperate to do something with his life, to make one final effort to leave something of himself behind. His impulse was toward immortality, as is anyone's, though he wouldn't have been willing or able to speak of it in those terms. With Celia's blessing he quit his wretched job selling chemical supplies to hotel chains and put the family's savings into a one-hour photo developing business, a great location in a busy strip mall in the suburbs, next to a popular buffet restaurant, lots of foot traffic, the place would practically run itself. The creep who sold him the business assured him it was a cash cow. You set up the developing chemicals in the back room, you kept the machines oiled and serviced, you put on a cheery smile every time a customer walked in the door, what could be simpler? People loved to take pictures, they loved to get them developed, they loved their memories frozen like that, everything perfect, the day at the beach, the ride on the roller coaster, the merry-go-round, Sundays at Grandma's, graduation day, first communions, Bar Mitzvahs, the picnic on the July Fourth, everything about it was a total can't-fail no-brainer, don't waste your time worrying about this one, you're home free.

The first two years were a dream. Celia quit her clerical job and came to work at the store. Yes, it was true, the hours were killing, and they were too old to be doing this kind of thing, but what else did they have to do? The house was so empty, and neither one of them had developed hobbies to pass the time. So they worked, side by side, they made business decisions together, they hired and fired, they toyed with the idea of opening a second store. Then Celia happened to spot an advertisement for a new kind of a camera, something called a digital camera—you could take your own pictures with it, and print them out on your own Apple computer. No film, no developing costs, no nothing. Who needed one-hour film developing when they didn't even need film anymore? Sure enough, by the end of the year the one-hour photo business was floundering, and by the end of the next year, they'd had to lay off every worker, even those who'd been with the store for several years. One fellow wept and clutched Celia's sleeve, begging. Another grew threatening, muttered darkly about torching the place, but did nothing. Eventually Wachtel sold the equipment, the chemicals, the display units, his inventory of film and photographic equipment—everything went. He got pennies on the dollar, walked away with his head in his hands. Celia, at her age, took a job as a file clerk at a bank. They stopped speaking to one another. Wachtel was alone in his life, and she was alone in her life, too. They lived like that, isolated from one another, for years. She'd suffered, and he'd suffered. And for what? So that now he could stand in the lobby of a hospital and make a scene with his brother-in-law, that criminal? This was what his life had come to?

"You showed up, Celia died," he told Cheeky. He couldn't help himself. "She was holding her own. She had life left in her."

"You said yourself the doctors gave her a week."

"So a week, then! A week! That's something!"

Cheeky sniffed and looked away. "Stay away from me," said Wachtel. "You come near me, I don't know what I'll do."

"C'mon, Stanley. Let's have dinner together."

"You just had a cup of tea and a cheese danish."

"I'm hungry. What can I tell you? Grief does strange things to a guy."

"So go get yourself something to eat."

"I thought maybe we could get a bite together."

"You ate plenty of meals the past forty years, you never called us and said let's go have dinner."

"I'm trying to make up for that now."

"You're too late."

"I know a great place. C'mon. My treat."

"Five minutes ago you didn't have a place to stay!"

"These people owe me." Cheeky put a hand on Wachtel's shoulder. "Let me do this. It's all I can do. I can't do anything for Celia anymore. You can't do anything for her either. But don't you think she would have wanted the two of us to break bread together after she was gone? Wouldn't she have wanted that?"

The Danforth Grill, Kansas City's oldest restaurant, occupied a walnut-paneled warren of rooms just off the marble-tiled lobby of the sumptuous Danforth Hotel, which had seen every President since William McKinley pass through its doors. This was old money, the kind of place Wachtel had spent a lifetime avoiding. Who needed this kind of aggravation? What kind of honest work was there in the world that paid out bucks sufficient for this kind of luxury? He'd heard about the Danforth Grill, had seen their ads occasionally on television. A Kansas City Tradition since 1890, and so on. Aged black waiters in crisp white dinner jackets, men who'd waited tables at the Danforth Grill since their youth, who'd grown old carrying platters of iced oysters on the half shell to pink-cheeked swells in country club attire—that sort of place. The menu was unchanged from the 1930s: cracked crab, oysters Rockefeller, grilled lobster with drawn butter, rack of lamb with those funny white chef's hats stuck on the end of each rib bone. Steak Diane, caesar salad, crepes Suzette, all of them done table side with great skill and flourish, flames jumping into the air. He'd thought of taking Celia and Arnie here once, when the scholarship from Berkeley came through, but Arnie nixed the idea—the Danforth Grill represented everything he despised in American culture, he informed his parents—and a good thing he had, too, because who had the money for this kind of extravagance? They'd gone to Shakey's for pizza instead.

He pulled up in the temporary parking zone in front of the hotel and immediately a uniformed black fellow opened the driver's side door. "Welcome to the Danforth Hotel," the man said in a soft, refined tone. "Will you be dining with us tonight?"

"Ask him," Wachtel said, pointing a thumb at Cheeky.

The attendant handed him a slip of paper, and another black fellow, this one younger but no less elegant in his uniform, slid behind the wheel, and in a moment the car was gone. "Don't you worry," the older black fellow said to Wachtel, noticing the look on his face. "Latrelle will take very good care of your car."

"Did you hear that? Where do they get these names?" Cheeky muttered as they walked through the heavy, brass-plated revolving door into the hotel's lobby.

"I'm not dressed for this," Wachtel said. "Look at me. What are we doing here? This place is formal. I'm wearing—I don't even have a tie."

"Would you just leave this to me?"

A small crowd, elegantly dressed, mostly couples, milled around the maître d's lectern, where a sallow, middle-aged man with a boutonniere in his lapel anxiously scrutinized a thick ledger, shaking his head and frowning. A trim young man nearby fielded phone calls on a cell phone. "No, I'm sorry," the young man said. "We're totally booked. The entire evening. It's Valentine's Day, you know." He clicked off, and the phone rang again immediately. "No, not this evening," he said. "I'm terribly sorry, Mr. Kemper. We always love to see you. But tonight it's simply impossible. We're booked to the rafters. Not an empty table all night."

"You hear that?" Wachtel whispered to Cheeky. "They're booked. It's Valentine's Day."

"Let me ask you something, Stanley," Cheeky said. "Have you ever tucked into Shrimp Newberg made by a professional, somebody who knows what they're doing, damn the calories, full speed ahead?"

"No. I haven't. And I'm not going to."

"Says you." Cheeky pushed his way to the maître d's lectern, pulling Wachtel behind him by the sleeve. "Excuse me!" he said to the maître d'. "My good man."

The man behind the lectern pushed his reading glasses down on his nose and gazed at Cheeky. "Yes?"

"Okay. I know you're booked for dinner tonight. But I was—" Cheeky began.

"Yes, we're booked all evening. I'm sorry."

"Is that right?"

"I'm afraid so." The maître d' shrugged apologetically and went back his intense study of the thick ledger spread out on the lectern.

"See, the thing is," said Cheeky, "my brother-in-law here just lost his wife. My sister, Celia. She died today." There was an audible catch in his voice. "Valentine's Day, if you can believe that. They've been married sixty years—longer. He's a wreck. He's... distraught."

"I'm terribly sorry."

"So here's what I'm thinking. You've got a table free. I know you do. You know it, I know it. There's a table back there. Little table back by the kitchen, I bet."

The maître d' lifted the ledger and held it out to Cheeky. It looked like an old-fashioned accounting ledger. "Tell me if you see any free tables, sir," the man said. His voice was cold now, brittle as ice.

"You idiot," Wachtel said into Cheeky's ear. "Can we get the hell out of here?"

"Give me a minute!" said Cheeky, and then turned back to the maître d'. "Get Ricardo out here. Tell him Cheeky wants to say hello."

"Ricardo's off this evening. Sir, we're fully booked."

"This is a nightmare," Wachtel said. He said this to the ceiling, which was beautifully painted, panels of a light, airy blue bisected by beams of mustard yellow. "I just want to go home. I want to be by myself. My wife just died." It was as if he were talking directly to God.

Cheeky pulled out his wallet, which was tattered and old. He withdrew a twenty-dollar bill. "The man's wife just died. Are you absolutely positive you don't see a table you could give us tonight?"

"Please. Put your money away. We're booked. There's nothing I can do."

Cheeky rolled the bill into a cigar. "Do you know who I am?" he demanded. "I'm Cheeky Mandelbaum! That name mean anything to you?"

"No sir, I'm afraid it doesn't."

"Time was, I could have walked in here, snapped my fingers, you'd have put us at the best table in the house. Like that!" He snapped his fingers for theatrical effect.

"Sir?" the maître d' said. "You're going to have to step away from the lectern. There are others waiting to speak to me."

Cheeky turned around. There were, indeed, several well-dressed patrons standing behind him, and he stared at them until their gazes shifted uneasily toward the door. He turned back to the lectern. "Okey-dokey," Cheeky said. "Number one, I'm finished with this place. You can forget about my patronage. Number two, you're not so fancy. I've eaten at places that make this joint look like a toilet. And number three—you never knew my sister, but let me tell you something. She was a great person. Make a long story short, we went our separate ways a long time ago, but when she was little she was something else."

"I'm going to have to ask you to stand aside," the maître d' said.

"You don't get it, do you! You little prick! I'm Cheeky Mandelbaum!"

The young man with the cell phone, who'd watched the exchange between Cheeky and his supervisor with an open mouth, leaned over to Wachtel. "Take him home or something, will you?" he asked. "I don't want to call the police. Take him someplace, buy him a drink."

"You stay out of this," Wachtel said. "What do you know about it." Suddenly he felt indignant, as if they'd made a reservation and now were being denied their table. "You people," he said, and then he stopped. What people? He couldn't help himself: he thought of

Arnie, and immediately a hole bloomed in the middle of his heart, the same black hole he'd felt every day of his life since his son's tragic disappearance. This hole had its own specific gravity, the force of a vacuum cleaner, and now it threatened to suck him into its nothingness, into the absence of everything, the darkness which was its essence. This was the day of Celia's death. Shouldn't he be somewhere sitting on a stool, tearing his clothing? Shouldn't he be weeping, blowing his nose, chanting the prayer for the dead? Instead, here he was, standing among strangers in a restaurant where he and Celia had never eaten, where they'd never even come to gawk at how the other half lived.

He put a firm hand on Cheeky's shoulder. "Cheeky. C'mon. We're leaving," he said.

The lighting at Town Topic on Broadway managed to be both dim and garish at the same time. How did they do that? Wachtel wondered about this as he ate his hamburger with grilled onions at the counter. He'd never seen anything like it anywhere. Cheeky, sitting beside him, was too busy shoving his double cheeseburger into his face to notice the lighting in this greasy spoon, or anything else about the place, for that matter—the thick haze of grease and cigarette smoke in the air, the semi-derelict elderly couple in a booth by the window sipping tea and sharing a pastry, or the big blank-faced white-blonde fellow at the other end of the counter, his hair twisted into corn rows, a blood-red tattoo snaking up the side of his face. He was wolfing down a double order of french fries doused in ketchup, humming to himself as he ate. Cheeky took enormous bites of his double cheeseburger, barely swallowing one before putting the next in his mouth, but seemed oddly unaware of the food itself, as if he might be feeding it to someone else, not himself. They were only a few blocks south of the Danforth Grill, though this seemed like a different city, a different world. It was darker here; the lighting seemed more menacing.

A pale young woman with a sleeping infant in her arms came in, and the cook, a bone-thin black man wearing a brightly colored knit scullcap, came around the counter to embrace her. "When'd you get out?" he asked her. He peeled back the shawl covering the infant's head and beamed at the puckered, sleeping face, its features dark and drawn into a scowl.

"Just today," she said.
"I get off at one. I'll stop by."
"I'll be up."

Wachtel watched all of this, listened to it, imagined the life this young couple might have, the husband a short-order cook at this dive, the woman just out—what, just out of jail? Just off work? No, who was he trying to kid, it was jail, no doubt about it, just released today, something minor, just a week or two behind bars and now she's free again. Who could tell if they were married? They had a child together—this was what Wachtel surmised, this scowling infant was theirs together. The young woman's face already bore the weight, the gravity of failure, a burden Wachtel knew only too well. Her eyes were heavy and dark-rimmed, and the lines bracketing her mouth were deeply etched. He wasn't the philosophical type. He didn't have the time or the inclination to ruminate on the meaning of life, had never given himself the chance to think about the big questions. That was Rabbi Silberberg's territory. Wachtel had always thought of the big questions as nothing more than the mud that children played with on a rainy day. Arnie had played in the mud as a child, making mud castles and then letting the rain wash them away to nothing. Wachtel had no time for such nonsense. But on the day of his wife's death, the day his life had turned, was still in the process of turning, into something new, something darker and grimmer than anything he'd ever known before, he allowed himself the momentary luxury of considering the imponderables. He thought of Celia in her dress, the Tip Top Tap Room, that dress, blue, something silky, so many years ago, it could have weighed two ounces, so long ago when everything seemed possible. What could it have meant, all their years together? What could it have possibly signified? If they'd known it would all come down to this, would they have fallen in love? Would they have bothered to dance at all?

He watched the pale young woman with the infant walk out the door, watched the short order cook gaze at them for a moment, his bony face blank with longing, before turning back to the grill. They understood already what was at stake, this young couple. Whatever innocence they'd been born with was gone, and they saw the world clearly, Wachtel imagined. Good for them. Let them figure it out now, while they're young and strong. He'd waited his whole life to understand what was happening to him, and even now, an old man with dewlaps and dentures, he felt he didn't have a clue.

When the cook slid their check down the counter toward them, Cheeky looked away. Wachtel pushed the check—the total came to just over eight dollars—toward him. "You wanted to buy me dinner," he said. "So buy."

Cheeky studied his nails. "That other place," he said after a moment, "I know some people there. Ricardo, he's the pastry chef, we go back a long way. I knew him back east. We were in business together for a while. You and me, we could have had dinner on the house."

"I don't care about any of that. Pay up. I saw that twenty you flashed at the maître d'."

"I don't know where I put it." Cheeky made a show of patting his pockets.

"You've got some *chutzpah*. You were a con artist when you were a kid, and you're a con artist now."

"Con artist! I'm ninety years old," said Cheeky. "I got peripheral naropathy! You know what that is? Everything hurts! I'm all played out. It's been a long day. I'm upset!"

"You're upset," Wachtel said.

"My sister died! Stake me to a cheeseburger for crissake, will you?"

Wachtel sucked on his dentures as he pulled a ten dollar bill out of his wallet. He laid it carefully on the counter, and called the short order cook over. "Keep the change." He watched carefully as the cook took the bill, rang up the sale, and put the change into a glass jar by the register.

Outside, the air had turned blustery again. The air was thin and brittle. Spring seemed a year away, though the weatherman on TV, that putz, kept saying each night that it would be arriving in five weeks, maybe sooner. This was a bad neighborhood; there was no use in denying it. Trash was piled in the gutters. Garbage. Somewhere nearby, a dog barked angrily. Across the street, a dark woman stood beneath a streetlight under a sign that advertised a school specializing in air conditioner repair courses. Her dress was torn at the shoulder, and she looked exhausted, punch-drunk, as if she'd just gone five rounds with someone.

"This is where we say goodbye," Wachtel said. He thought about going home, about turning the key and walking into the house alone. What was that going to be like? What was anything going to be like now that Celia was dead? For years the house had been haunted not only by the ghost of Arnie, but the ghost of their dreams for him and for themselves. Now there would be Celia's ghost wandering the hallways as well, making noise in the night. He held out a hand to Cheeky. He didn't want to do it, but Celia would have wanted him to. Shake the man's hand and be done with it. It was an empty gesture, anyway. What was a handshake? It was nothing. It meant nothing. It was one of those things we all did out of habit. One of the tribes Arnie had lived with for a time in New Guinea while he researched his first book said goodbye to each other by laughing hysterically, falling on the ground, kicking their feet as if in the midst of a fit of some kind. Wachtel stared at his hand, but Cheeky didn't take it.

"Put me up for the night," Cheeky said. He looked away. His chin was quivering. Wachtel could see it in the dim light of a streetlamp. The man was on the verge of tears again.

"One night," said Cheeky. "That's all I'm asking."

"You've got to be kidding."

"I'm ninety years old, Stanley. We're *mizpuchah*. We're family. You got a spare room? It'd be a *mitzvah*."

"Don't give me that *mispuchah* crap. Don't talk *mitzvahs* with me. My wife just died. I need some time to myself. Don't you have any pity in you?"

"I got plenty of pity."

"Yeah, for yourself you got plenty. Ninety years old! I saw you put away that burger."

"I shouldn't have eaten it. My gut's ruined. That stuff's going to kill me."

"So why'd you eat it, then? Who put a gun to your head?"

A long pause ensued. Finally Cheeky said, "I don't know what to tell you. Can you put me up for the night or not? If you can't do it, you can't do it. Just drop me off at the mission on your way home."

"What mission? What are you talking about?"

"I don't know. Any mission."

"How'm I supposed to know where there's a mission? You think I hang out with bums?"

"Just drop me off."

"Do you ever know what you're talking about?"

"Now you're making me mad," Cheeky said. "You're insulting my intelligence."

"To hell with your intelligence. A lot of good it did you. My son, Arnie, could think rings around you. He scored perfect 800s on his SATs."

"I know. I read about it in the paper. In the *Kansas City Star*. It made the front page."

"You read about it, you didn't think to call us up? You were too good to drop by and pay your respects to your sister?"

"That was a long time ago. Things were different."

"You didn't think, 'That's my nephew'? You didn't think, 'Maybe I'll write him a card, tell him congratulations from his Uncle'?"

"I thought about it." Cheeky turned away and coughed wetly into a cupped fist. "You ever think I might have been ashamed?" he asked. "That ever occur to you?" When he turned back to face Wachtel, his eyes were glittering.

"All right, then. One night," said Wachtel with a groan. He was overcome by a wave of pity, suddenly awash in it, drowning, scarcely able to breathe.

The house was cold. He'd left the thermostat set at sixty-seven that morning. There was mail in the foyer, shoved through by the postman. Bills. Thank God they had insurance. The house was paid for, he had a Blue Cross/Blue Shield policy that filled in the gaps in Medicare, and after the second business failed, he and Celia had managed to eke out a living from the scraps of their savings and Social Security put together. A Mexican woman came once a week to mop and vacuum, so the place looked okay. It smelled like old people, Wachtel knew that, he couldn't help it. He didn't know what he meant by that: the cleanser he used on his dentures; moldy cheese; furniture polish. It smelled old, but it was an old house, and not in good repair, to be honest about it. Anyway, he felt at home here; it was where they'd raised their son; their lives were in the walls of this place, bound up in the carpeting, the furniture, the drapes. In the kitchen, to the left of the window that looked over the back yard, hung a cast iron medallion that read, "The opinions expressed by the husband of this house are not necessarily those of the management." Celia had bought that at a craft fair in Sedalia forty-five years ago, and it had hung there by the window ever since. Wachtel had never liked it, had been tempted to take it down and throw it away on more than one occasion, and now he considered the possibility of getting rid of the thing at last. Then he realized that he'd come to love it. Who could explain such a thing?

"Your room's down the hall," he said to Cheeky. "It was Arnie's room."

"I really appreciate this, Stan," said Cheeky. "I get back on my feet I'm going to pay you back for this. Every penny."

"Shut up about that. I don't want to hear any of it." He led Cheeky into Arnie's old bedroom and turned on the bedside reading lamp. The room looked exactly as it had for the past forty-five years: a narrow single bed, its navy blue coverlet straight and flat as an iron; a tattered, multi-colored oval hooked rug, a crafts project Arnie had completed in the Cub Scouts; a Gustav Klimt poster on one wall; a framed black and white portrait of the Beatles on another. The chest of drawers was empty, as was the drawer of the small student's desk in the corner. Arnie's electric typewriter still sat at the ready, though—the lightweight Corona he'd been given as a graduation gift by the principal of his high school and had carried with him through Berkeley and Michigan. He'd written his dissertation on this typewriter, then the book. Every once in a while over the years, after Arnie had disappeared and hope for his return had faded away, Wachtel had come in here and turned on the machine, listened to its quiet, steady hum for a moment or two before turning it off and shutting the door again. It was as close as he could come to communing with the dead boy, as close as he allowed himself to anything that smacked of sentimentality.

Cheeky landed hard on the bed. In the warm glow of the bedside lamp, he looked ruddy, but Wachtel could see that the man was on the verge of collapse. "Get some sleep," he said. "In the morning we'll talk."

"I need some help."

"We'll talk in the morning."

"No, I mean now—I need some help right now." With some effort, Cheeky pulled the velcro tabs on his shoes and slid his feet free. He rolled down his socks, which were white and full of holes. His feet were awful. Two toes on the right foot were black, three on the left were a deep brown. The rest of the flesh was a pasty white, mottled by angry red welts. Exposed to the air, they suddenly smelled like rotten meat.

"Jesus Christ," said Wachtel. "What's wrong with you?"

"I don't know." Cheeky looked at his feet impassively, a blank stare, as if he didn't actually see them. "I get a cut or something, a blister, it don't heal."

"Doesn't it hurt, for crissake?"

"Everything hurts. I told you already. Peripheral naropathy."

"You got diabetes or something?"

"I don't know. It runs in the family. My brother Julius had it, I think." He shrugged. "I don't remember. We're out of touch."

"You're a grown man, you're supposed to take care of yourself. You've seen a doctor?"

"How'm I going to see a doctor? To hell with them. Bunch of high and mighty pricks. Overpaid plumbers."

"Tomorrow I'll call around, try to get you in to see somebody."

"Says you. I don't want to go to a doctor."

"Well, you're going. You don't watch out, you're going to lose your feet, you know that? We'll have to sell you to the circus. Cheeky Mandelbaum, the guy with no feet."

"You trying to scare me, don't bother. I don't scare so easy."

"I'm trying to get you some help, you dumb ox. You need help."

"I don't need anything."

Celia had soaked her feet in Epsom salts from time to time, and there was a box of the stuff, plus the basin she used for the soaking, under the sink in the bathroom down the hall. "Okay. Wait a minute," Wachtel said. "I'll get you something that'll make you feel better. Just hold your horses." He went down the hall to the bathroom, squatted on painful knees in front of the sink, and retrieved the basin and the box of Epsom salts. He read the instructions on the back (Celia had always done this for herself, even near the end, when her breath came in gasps and she could no longer handle stairs). He took the basin into the kitchen, where the sink was bigger, and filled it with hot water, sprinkled in the Epsom salts, then he lifted the basin carefully and carried it into Cheeky's room. It was heavy, the cloudy water moved in waves; he walked slowly, aware of every step, every swing of his hips.

"Here you go," he said, and put the basin down by Cheeky's feet. He'd tried to be careful, but despite his efforts a little of the water sloshed out onto the hooked rug by the bed. "Soak in this awhile. It'll make you feel better."

"What's that?" Cheeky said.

"Epsom salts."

"What the hell is that supposed to do?"

"Put your feet in. You'll thank me."

Cheeky hesitated. "That water's hot," he complained.

"Of course it's hot. It's supposed to be hot. Put your feet in there, you'll feel like a million bucks."

"I can't lift my feet."

"What do you mean, you can't lift your feet. You were walking two minutes ago."

"I'm tired."

"You're tired," said Wachtel, and slowly, not without pain, he sank to his knees on the hooked rug. "All right," he said. "Now just relax." He gently lifted Cheeky's feet, first one and then the other, into the basin. "There. That ought to feel pretty good."

Cheeky winced. "I told you that water was too hot," he said through clenched teeth.

"Ah, for the love of Mike. Will you ever shut up?" Wachtel had meant the question to come out gruffly, but the tone of his voice was soft and bone-weary, more like a plea, like a prayer at the end of a very long day.

ALEXIS WIGGINS

Unanimal

Twenty years old, sparkly makeup on my eyes and cheeks, I wrap a leg over the back of my uncle's motorcycle, hoist myself onto the cracked vinyl seat.

He's the cool uncle. The uncle who's fifteen years older than me, who dates a model, who sips tequila from wide-mouthed glasses in Chelsea bars. Who gives me advice as we drink my grandparents' wine out on the front stoop, advice like: Why buy the cow when you get the milk for free? Which means: What motivation does Richard have to take you out for a nice dinner when you're already sleeping with him? I make a face at my uncle when he says this, a face like he doesn't know what he's talking about, but, after, I look away, down the West Village street, wondering if he's right.

On the back of the bike, I can't help but think, smug and superior, how just a few nights ago I had my legs wrapped around Richard. The same ones now wrapped around the 1979 Motto Guzzi, clicking and humming its way over the Brooklyn Bridge, as June night air runs its fingers through my hair.

Tonight my uncle takes me to Slick's, his bike man's place deep in Brooklyn. Slick is black. He's tall, older than my parents. He lives among grease and cranks, screws and rags with smudge marks all over them. I don't know where he sleeps. Slick has five or six Rotweillers milling around him. They growl at me intermittently, like they can't decide whether I'm a friend or a thief.

Slick and my uncle go off to talk bikes, and I'm left with the dogs. Without Slick, the dogs get wilder. They paw me, bare their teeth, take the edge of my t-shirt in their mouths and pull. They growl, guttural and low. They begin to hop up, digging their paws, like the feet of antique tables, into my belly. I'm scared. "Slick," I call meekly. The sound of my voice makes one of the dogs bark, a sharp sound. The other dogs sense her angst; they start circling, white teeth flashing like pearls. One of them closes her mouth over my hand, and I feel the edges of her teeth making marks in my skin. I call again, filled like a water pitcher with fear. "Slick!" He emerges from another room, from shadows and shelves full of metal things. "Git!" he hisses, and the dogs scatter. "Git!" he yells again as they trot by him. He raps one of them on the nose as she passes, and she scampers away, tail between her legs; the others follow—the sound of claws on cement. I'm safe.

So why can't I relax? Why can't I breathe a sigh of relief once we leave Slick's and head home? Why am I sullen on the ride back? Why does the night air now whip my face, the city lights from the Brooklyn Bridge seem blurry and rinsed out? Why can't I muster up anything but dread when I call Richard, find him at home, slink over to his place? Why can't I get the image of those dogs, their hot, wet breath against my skin, out of my mind when Richard and I are naked in bed?

Because they knew. They could smell it on me, I think as I lie there, Richard inside me, my face turned to the wall. Those dogs could smell how little I wanted to be fucked and how much I wanted to be loved, and they hated me for not doing anything about it. *You're not an animal,* they said. *We don't even know what you are.*

I know, I want to say. I am unfit for the animal kingdom, sparkly makeup on my face, legs wrapped around this man. I'm not a cow. Not even a bitch.

JULIE SUK

Flying Through World War I

His plane was scarcely more than canvas
stretched across board.

Gunned down by a German Fokker onto no-man's land,
my father crawled under cross-fire to a crater
and sprawled in on the dead.

Only once did he mention the maggots and stench
in a world that slammed up too soon.

That night, between the sizzle of flares,
a Yank pulled him back into a trench, and left
before the swapping of names.

Long after I came and went my ways, a friend of his
passed through town, bringing with him an army pal.
Buddy, old buddy, war tales told until what do you know—
true, I swear true—they found it was the stranger
who'd rescued my father.

Crying, they embraced—life is so sweet!
when death is on leave.

By spring a tumor invaded my father's brain,
taking him out, along with his wish to float
once just once again with the noiseless clouds.

I'm left replaying those summer nights
we sat on the stoop, bull-bats diving overhead,
cicadas puncturing the quiet.

See, he pointed, there—there! scorpion,
fish, ram and lyre, wheeling across a sky
threatened by hunter and bear.

Hiding my face on his arm, it was hard to connect
myth with the lap I nestled in.

And still no clue
from a heaven seemingly preoccupied.

Tracers that stutter around us
briefly illuminate our lives,

what I forgot to say, what I forgot to give
to the living, bringing me down to a fragment
of you, my derring-do father who flew.

Babcia

White-haired, stolid madonna wrapped in shawls
crocheted by hand, waits stately in the chair,
hands folded, and seems to stare straight through the walls.

Perhaps she looks because she finds things there,
inside the bumps and grooves of textured paint:
Poland, husband, country house, the air

draping the mountain in the summer, faint
with the scent of pine. Perhaps the war, the camps
so close to home, the ashes that would taint

the streets she crossed to buy her lettuce, stamps,
fresh butter. Mother of these ghosts that mill
around her, she sits quiet by the lamp.

An amber glass sweats by her on the table.
Her son makes sure that glass is always full.

DAVID TUCKER

The House

The turning of the pages of a magazine
in the middle of a morning sends
waiting-room echoes through the quiet house,
echoes that are making us old.

The routines that hold us closer to them
and this sense that steady notice is being taken
of us somewhere now, this is making us old
and the objects with us for so many years
the way they watch the changes to our skin
and voices, listening for repeated stories,
the books that eye us and glance
sidelong at each other, the yawns declaring themselves
a little louder and coffee being poured,
sounding harsher because the house is quieter
by degrees, all this makes us old.

And the weather that has been light
and blue for weeks is also making us old.
Years of love have made us old, lovemaking
in all our different beds and houses,
the painstaking care of children,
sleepless nights, work and promises
have made us old. I touch your hand
in the night, your sleeping face,
and we still make promises about the future
but smile about what we can't stop.

Thin clouds skim across the moon.
Nights are cool with a little wind.
We leave the windows open
and more old age comes in.

Three Abominations

It must be just bad translating, like *Robot Chicken* and *Fly Head;* but thoughts of the three—
Walnut tumors? Moo shu pus? Fire-bombed
baby with broccoli?—make my hunger high-
tail it like Iron Man in a thunderstorm.

The *Pair of Love Shrimp* moan syphilitically.
Seafood Commissioner takes bribes to okay
rancid clams. The *Sauteed Happy Family
in a Basket* could be Mom, Dad, Sis, and me.
Yet my old favorites—*Sweet-and-Sour Pork,*

Kung Pao Chicken, Mongolian Beef—seem
cowardly. I've never ever snorted meth, fizzled
fart-sounds when a fat lady sat, or slept
with anyone I didn't love. How can I settle
for *Three Heavenly Flavors, Milky Way Eggplant,*

or *Pork in Soothing Lettuce* when I dream
of being, not Hard-Working Model Husband
and Father of Three, but Biker Ex-Con Sire
of Thirty by Thirty, blowing down the freeway,
flipping off Honda Civics just like mine?

I'm alone in a cathouse-red leather booth
three thousand miles from home. Genghis
Khan's blood thundering through his veins,
the waiter asks for my order.
                                  What will it be?

What Kitty Knows

In the same week that John F. Kennedy, Jr., with wife
Caroline and her sister Lauren, crashed his private plane
into the sea, a Kentuckian who worked for Tyson Foods—

which gave big money to President Bill Clinton, who led
the mourning for JFK, Jr.—fell into, not a vat, *vat* sounds
undignified, like in that old song, "I Fell Into a Vat

of Chocolate"; so call it a vast *container*, a *cauldron*
of chicken "parts" being cooked into cat food. And this man—
given three column-inches because death-by-cat-food

struck some editor as cute—this un-named man was boiled/
drowned/asphyxiated by *9 Lives*. Hey—if half a can
in my cat's dish can make dinner rise in my stomach

like the masses in revolt, what would a whole vast, steaming
cauldron do? Anyway, in the same week John Jr.—
"John-John," "World's Handsomest Man," as close to royalty

as the U.S.A. has got—was gracing more front pages
than he did after his touching-even-if-rehearsed salute
as the caisson hauling his dead dad clattered by, Mr. No-Name,

Mr. Hillbilly-Twang, Mr. Loved-A-Sixer-After-Work,
who maybe thought pro wrestling is real, and Oprah,
an intellectual, and watched *America's Vilest Home Videos*

to see the world's fattest (812 pounds) model, the leech-
sucking boy, and the Icelandic girl who made her wedding
dress from frozen spit—this man who probably roared

(I did!) to see that zoo-keeper's head sucked literally up
an elephant's nether eye, Mr. Zip O. Zilchinsky plunged
into Snowball's breakfast/Mitten's lunch/Fluffy's din-din, died,

and had to share his three column-inches with No-Name Two,
who tried to save him—a friend maybe, or some Security guy
paid to risk his life like those Secret Service Men who failed

to save John-John's dad. In any case, Two tried a rescue,
and "overcome by methane," dropped the rope, plunged into the
    stew,
and wasn't laughing, I can tell you, when Death's Big Chicken

pecked up his life-line like a worm. Our country spent millions
to fish out its crashed prince; but I wonder, is it normal
kitty smugness that I see in Matt the Cat's green tiger-eyes,

or some just-ingested knowledge that Man is no Immortal, and
    not
worthy to drag him from his warm sofa into a night comfortless
and cold as the bottom of the sea?

ALAN WILLIAMSON

For My Mother

We refused to obey the law and scatter your ashes
a full mile offshore: you had asked for the tiderocks—

chain of islets, really, off the point, where the sea explodes
most crystalline; but walkable at low water—

after a handful were buried on my father's grave.
What childhood foot-memory kept me steady, the square

cornered box off-weighting my arms, thrown by the rocks'
tilted faces and blunt points—the hot March sun—

(But why the tiderocks? They were my place, not yours,
where our biologist friend named the new species

of nudibranch we found there, alanii; yet I remember you there,
sunrise-touched, uncharacteristically happy

for that summer we had to go West,
my father in the hospital; Liberty scarf round your hair—

Did you think of that, too?) The rocks' cracks and trapezoidal
jumble, revealed in the photo, a kind of grid

or graph paper to map our bent-over shapes, hair-fine—
against time, against life?—out to the far tooth

where I cast the last ashes aslant the wind, to fall
only half in water, half dusting

a nest of barnacles, to wait for the high tide...
Another mistake, desecration? As when I left you

the day I shouldn't, gambling the doctors were right, no change,
your premonition wrong... The others

don't blame me, of course; and what
could it matter now, anyway?

All I can ever do for you is done.

IRENE WILLIS

You Want It?

Here, take it,
my mother would say,
unwinding a scarf
from her neck,
slipping off a bracelet,
a ring too small for my finger
she tried to force anyway.
A giver, a couldn't-hold-
on-to-it, my mother was.
She would give you,
as they say, the shirt
off her back—and ours.
My father's three-piece
suit and gray fedora, my
white embroidered sweater,
last year's coat, and once,
three jackets, lowered
on the dumbwaiter when
the super needed clothes.
A fiver for the insurance
man, out of cigars. Hazel,
my mother's friend, got me
for lessons on an out-of-tune
piano while her out-of-work
husband sat in my father's
pants and watched.

ABOUT B. H. FAIRCHILD

A Profile by Rebecca Morgan Frank

On a rainy day in Claremont, California, you might find B. H. Fairchild drafting a poem and drinking a double espresso in the second seat of the front window of Some Crust Bakery. Other days, you might find him writing in a little place behind his garage. Officially, "B. H." stands for "Bertram Harry," a family name shared by his father and grandfather, though Fairchild most often answers to "Pete." The story behind his name, like many of Fairchild's stories, involves his father: having lobbied for a simpler name, the elder Bertram returned from World War II to find his wife had caved under her mother-in-law's pressure to uphold family tradition; Fairchild's father insisted they ignore the birth certificate and use "Pete" instead.

In the afterward of his second book, *Local Knowledge*, Fairchild describes this early memory of his father: "As a child in West Texas, I am standing beside my father as he works a machine lathe at a shop in one of several dusty oilfield towns." For Fairchild, the memory "holds the model for everything I have written, especially poems: lathework." And lathework remains, after five books, the presiding model for his poetic work. "It's lodged so deeply in my subconscious," he says, "that it could hardly be otherwise. If poetry weren't such a demanding craft, requiring steady attention to detail, to what most people regard as small matters, I probably wouldn't have any interest in it. As I've said before, if there's an easy way to write poems, I don't want to know about it."

Born in Houston, and raised in small oil towns in Kansas, Texas, and Oklahoma, Fairchild is the child of parents who were the children of small farmers. His father quit high school to help support his parents and siblings by working as a lathe machinist, and he continued this work while raising his own children, often taking the younger Fairchild with him to the shops. Those machine shops and the communities around them deeply influenced Fairchild. He notes, "Ours was a fairly typical blue-collar family, though my parents worked very hard to pull us up into the middle class, to own their own home, to help send us to college—the story of an entire generation, I think."

Fairchild's poems resonate with the duality of that experience, of years growing up watching his father at work, and, later, of summers spent working alongside him during his years at the University of Kansas. There, Fairchild remembers, "poems of all kinds—from Shakespeare, Keats, Dickinson, Frost, Eliot, Snyder, Ginsberg, William Stafford—were happening to me all at once, so I tended to see less difference among them and more difference between the radical, unique thing called poetry and the rest of the world." Fairchild began to forge a bridge between those worlds, and that sensibility echoes through much of his work. In the title poem of *The Art of the Lathe*, Fairchild depicts a boy who is surrounded by both machine work and a created beauty infiltrating his environment:

> The boy leaves the shop, cringing into the light,
> and digs the grime from his fingernails, blue
> from bruises. Walking home, he hears a clavier—
> Couperin, maybe, a Bach toccata—from a window overhead.
> *Music*, he thinks, *the beautiful.*

> Tavern doors open. Voices. Grab and hustle of the street.
> Cart wheels. The room of his life. The darkening sky.

The world of the machinist repeatedly interfaces with experiences of music and art in the poems from this collection, such as in "Beauty," where the narrator stands beside his wife in front of Donatello's David and recalls the men of the machine shop, a connection that brings him to question the experience and naming of beauty. The narrator, in the opening of the poem, confesses "that no male member of my family has ever used / this word in my hearing or anyone else's except / in reference, perhaps, to a new pickup or a dead deer." And in "The Machinist, Teaching His Daughter to Play the Piano," the final line asserts how it is not only the poet, artist, or musician who inhabits both worlds, but also the working man who is "a master of lathes, a student of music."

Fairchild first began writing poems in high school, but these were, by his own admission, "terrible ones," and as an undergraduate, he wrote mostly fiction. Poetry came later: he began writing poems seriously in his twenties, and the poems of his first book date back to his thirties. After he completed his Ph.D. at the University of Tulsa, Fairchild moved right into teaching, sustaining a demanding load in order to support his family which grew to include two children. After twenty-five years of teaching nine and sometimes ten classes a year at California State University, Fairchild now commutes quite a distance to his position as the Lorraine Sherley Professor of American Literature at Texas Christian University, where he is able to teach, comparatively, much less. Of those earlier years he says, "Looking back, I'm really not sure how I got anything written, but I guess I did. It had a lot to do with writing at night, sometimes until three or four in the morning, and because of that, I still have bad sleep habits. I will say, with deep appreciation, that that university, along with some awards money I had won, helped me to take a year off, which was when I finally completed *Early Occult Memory Systems of the Lower Midwest*. It's amazing how much you can write when you actually have the time."

While somehow, even in those early days, Fairchild always found time for poems, the short life of a poetry press meant it took a while for those poems to be given rightful notice. Fairchild's first book, *The Arrival of the Future*, was originally published by Swallow's Tale Press, not long before they dissolved in 1985, leaving the collection essentially without a publisher. The second book was published in 1991 as part of the renowned *Quarterly Review of Literature* series, in which multiple poets were collected in one volume. It was an important publication, but easily overlooked as an individual work. So, in 1997, Fairchild's third book, *The Art of the Lathe*, entered the world in some ways like a debut. A very successful debut. As the winner of the Beatrice Hawley Award from Alice James Press, the collection garnered universal praise, winning the Kingsley Tufts Poetry Award, the William Carlos Williams Award, the PEN West Poetry Award, the California Book Award, the Natalie Ornish Poetry Award from the Texas Institute of Letters, and was named a finalist for the National Book Award.

The enthusiastic reception to *The Art of the Lathe* led to a revival of Fairchild's earlier work. Alice James opted to republish *The Arrival of the Future*, and, other than some proofreading and the addition of a preface and a few notes, Fairchild let his first book stand as such. "I thought it was important," he says, "that the poems in the first book appear unchanged (and I think this about all first books) as an accurate record of the poet's beginnings." Later, after publishing Fairchild's fourth book, *Early Occult Memory Systems of the Lower Midwest* (2003), W. W. Norton reprinted *Local Knowledge*. This time around, Fairchild did make structural changes. "I was likewise very happy when Norton offered to republish my second book," he says, "but for quite a different reason. I had begun to see that the structure of the book was all wrong and wanted to reshape it." Ever modest, Fairchild is quick to note his gratitude for all the support he has been given, and particularly for the door opened for him by Alice James Press.

The praise keeps coming for Fairchild. *Early Occult Memory Systems of the Lower Midwest* won the National Book Critics Circle Award, and the poem "Mrs. Hill" was included by Rita Dove in the *Best American Poems of 2000*. Numerous organizations have honored his work, including the National Endowment for the Arts, the Guggenheim Foundation, the Rockefeller Foundation, and the MacDowell Colony. His latest collection ventures into new territory, as Fairchild includes prose pieces written under a heteronym he describes as "one Roy Eldridge Garcia, a character in 'The Blue Buick' who is based upon about three different men I knew when I was working in the machine shop. Roy was in Paris during the fifties, so they are more or less typical of the sort of thing being written there then." In this scene from "The Blue Buick," it is evident that the men of the machine shops remain a powerful influence on Fairchild's life and work:

> and it was there full-volume when Roy came home
> from work and they began to dance, martinis in hand,
> and soon you were there in the Hot Club in Paris
> rather than a tiny Airstream trailer parked
> along the southern outskirts of Liberal, Kansas,
> where a boy, amazed, sat at a yellow formica
> breakfast table watching something that might be,
> he wondered, some form, some rare, lucky version,
> of human happiness.

More poems written in the guise of Roy Garcia will appear in Fairchild's fifth book, *Usher,* which is forthcoming from Norton. Fairchild reveals that the collection will include "a section of philosophical poems, or poems that arise from ideas or problems in philosophy, and a section dealing with the death of small towns in the Midwest." Another section, entitled "Trilogy," which Fairchild labels the "heart of the new book," will be published as a limited edition by PennyRoyal Press with illustrations by Barry Moser. For now, readers are left with the open ended closing passage of "The Memory Palace," the final poem in *Early Occult Memory Systems of the Lower Midwest.* Ending, as it does, with a simple colon implies a kind of promise, that endings are also beginnings for a poet like Fairchild, or a simple pact that there is more to come from this talented voice:

> But there's no more time, it's morning, time to go to work,
> and they are opening the huge shop door, the slow rumble
> that you will never forget, and the light leaking in, widen-
> ing—light like a quilt of gold foil flung out so it will drape all

of this, will keep it and keep it well—and it is so bright now, you can hardly bear it as it fills the door, this immense glacier of light coming on, and still you do not know who you are, but here it is, try to remember, it is all beginning:

Rebecca Morgan Frank is the editor and cofounder of Memorious: a journal of new verse and fiction.

BOOKSHELF

Books Recommended by Our Staff Editors

The Monsters of Templeton, *a novel by Lauren Groff* (Voice): What's fresh and fun about *The Monsters of Templeton*, by Lauren Groff, is how it doesn't fit neatly into one contemporary genre. It's literary, it's historical, and it's peppered with mysteries, ghosts, and "monsters." Even the packaging of the book is a delight—full of illustrations, family trees, and maps.

Graduate student Willie Upton returns home pregnant and disgraced by scandal on the same day that a dead, Loch Ness-style monster surfaces from the town's vast lake. Her hippie-turned-born-again mother, descended from Templeton's founding families, is newly compelled to finally tell Willie the truth: that Willie was not conceived during a San Francisco love-in, but is in fact the child of a fellow Templetonian. She refuses to say just who the man is, however, leaving archeologist Willie to research her way through two hundred years of town and family secrets.

Groff, like her digger protagonist, is interested in exploring what lies below surfaces, and she has no trouble dropping metaphor firmly into the story from the first sentence: the monster surfacing in the lake named Glimmerglass. Birth. Death. Her deft handling of multiple voices results in chapters that weave back and forth through time. Old letters, diary entries, even a portion of an eighteenth-century book appears, and what we learn about the past not only changes our take on it, it causes us to reflect on just what the past is, anyway. And yes, she flirts with the supernatural, but in a very Jamesian way—every incident of the uncanny in this story could also be argued as being psychological in origin.

Groff based Templeton and some of its inhabitants partly on her beloved hometown, Cooperstown, New York, and partly on the literary Templeton created by Cooperstown's own James Fenimore Cooper. Myths and characters she grew up with elbowed their way into the book she wanted to write, she says, as a "love story for Cooperstown."

The result is an accomplished debut, detailing a well-drawn world that a reader has no trouble settling into and believing in. Filtering through it is a yearning for the mysteries of childhood and at the same time, a desire for those mysteries not to be completely revealed. When Groff's prose is at its most lyrical, past and present fuse beautifully. An elderly doctor, in a boat, rowing around the dead lake creature, begins to weep:

> *In his mouth there was the sweet burn of horehound candy, the exact savor of his long-ago childhood.*

And one night Willie stays up for hours reading letters dating from the Civil War:

> *By the time I looked up, dazed, from the letters, and out the window into the dark and sleeping town, I saw another change. I felt as if I were rising out of my body, then through the roof, and when I looked down, there was a different Templeton, busy even in the earliest parts of the dawn. I could hear the sleeping regiments in the fields out by the river, the night watch's boots on the frozen ground.*

In her author's note, Groff quotes James Fenimore Cooper: "An interesting fiction...addresses our love of truth." *The Monsters of Templeton* is an interesting fiction indeed. —Maryanne O'Hara
Maryanne O'Hara is Associate Fiction Editor of Ploughshares.

National Anthem, p*oems by Kevin Prufer* (Four Way): Kevin Prufer's terrific fourth collection exposes a nightmare straight from the head of Walt Whitman. In it, America sings a democratic song of distress, with no one, or thing, denied suffering or a voice: not the moon, nor minor politicians, shopping centers or the book's most prevalent speaker, an 'I' without biography, who transcribes societal and environmental break-down via tropes suggestive of the post-apocalyptic scenarios of Mad Max and television's "Jericho," of the conquer-n-collapse history of the Roman age.

A little dissociated, sometimes bemused, always hyper-vigilant, the speakers of these poems often sing in hauntingly soft rhyme, a harmony that belies the dissonances within psyches both national and personal, as in "The Moon is Burning:" "I have often looked across the fields, and the moon said, / *You have only a short time, your kind.* I paid it no mind. / Everything is always / talking. Dark moon, crescent, half, afire, / moon that skimmed the distant mountains / beyond which the Capitol slept, // moon that reddened them—and cast the city, I guessed, / in a lovely glow."

Like "The Wasteland's" hysterical woman on a "burnished throne" and her distracted-by-dystopia partner, the you in "Those Who Could Not Flee" tries to engage a companion on edge over imminent destruction: "And you were saying, / *Why shouldn't we adopt? / A Chinese? A Romanian? A noble thing to do, these days,* / and if the buildings burned / we wouldn't see them through the weather // ...*A child from far away, a Russian / or a black one*... // They'd burn the city / and the ones who couldn't flee / they'd skin and nail to posts."

Prufer's America is a country populated by clueless victims of fashion (foreign adoption as "thing to do") and hyper-aware victims of dread, with serious communication between them impossible. That the nameless partner would continue to muse on the "nobility" of bringing children of foreign birth to a country on the verge of violent invasion is its own fatal commentary.

Here, as in other poems in the book's first section, the Roman Empire and the American one are inextricably conflated, the legions of Paulinas and "blue-faced" enemies inhabiting the same territory as the infamous Texas truck dragging case and the "they hate our freedoms" rationale for Islamo-terrorism. As in a contemporary Roman city, time in "National Anthem" exists in layers: a layered 'now' through which history reverberates, the past commingling with a dystopic present, empire collapsing, reconstituting and collapsing again in a loop of images by turns gorgeous, frightening and banal. In "What We Did With The Empire," two people do everything they can to be rid of it: hiding it in a sofa and leaving it "near the curb for students," burying it by a doghouse, even tying a barbell to it and throwing it over a bridge.

In the great "A History of the American West," the American West dreams on, a veritable Whitman sleeping "on an open raft...hat tipped forward...one hand limp...Gorgeous in his jeans and sunburnt arms, / gone / to the bomb blast and the gasp of time, / to Brigham Young and his wagonload of wives, / the heel and rein of men on horseback." Asleep to its reality of "fallout, cancer, birds trapped in the cloud," the Dust Bowl, even its own vulnerability, the American West "stall(s) in the brush...gone to everything but the gentle dream / in which the West rides westward" and the dream girls "who touch the horse's sweat-damp coat, who stroke the shank, the saddle, / and his thigh—" and who then, suddenly, even voraciously, "haul him down."

The book's second section is more intimate in scope, presenting the death of family and youth (girls, boys, the father) as a more personal analog to the empire collapse so vividly detailed in section one. Its strongest poems—"Girls in Heaven," "Cicada Shell," "Leukotomy"—display a wonderment of the surreal and the horrible that vivifies the entire book. But it's "National Anthem's" song of the imminent collapse of the American Empire that most thrilled and riveted this reader, and makes this book so memorable. —*Dana Levin*

Dana Levin's most recent book of poetry is Wedding Day *(Copper Canyon). A 2007 Guggenheim Fellow, she chairs the Creative Writing and Literature Department at College of Santa Fe.*

Every Past Thing, *a novel by Pamela Thompson* (Unbridled Books): I mean no slight to Pamela Thompson's dazzling first novel, *Every Past Thing*, when I say that here is a book that can be judged by its cover: A reproduction of Edwin Romanzo Elmer's exquisite "Mourning Picture." (The original hangs in the Smith College Museum of Art.) In the foreground, Elmer depicts his only daughter, Effie, with her pet sheep, Her Excellency, shortly before her death. In the background sit he and his wife, dressed in mourning, and half the size of their ten-year-old daughter. Just as there is nothing conventional about the painting, which portrays its subjects in proportion to emotional importance rather than physical size, so there is nothing conventional about Thompson's deeply imagined narrative.

The action of *Every Past Thing* takes place in New York City, in a single week of November 1899, during which various characters offer us fragments of a story that together form a fractured, and deeply moving, whole. Most particularly we get the point of view of Effie's mother, Mary, whose life has come to a standstill since her daughter's death and who is only now, as she and her husband move to New York so that Edwin can study art, awakening to the present. Drawn by her memories of Jimmy Roberts, a young man with whom she has had a brief intimacy and a long correspondence, Mary begins to visit a bar that he has mentioned his letters, a famous meeting place for anarchists and intellectuals.

While Mary sits drinking cider, writing and reordering her papers, she meets a young journalist who in turn introduces her to his sister. Frank and Susanna are immensely appealing characters both to Mary and to the reader but the story of their meetings and conversations forms only one strand of this complex narrative. In addition to Mary's point of view we also get glimpses of Edmund's struggles at art school, the relationship between Edmund and his much more successful brother Samuel, Samuel's relationship with Mary, and the love triangle that brought Mary to marry the brother she didn't care for rather than the one she did.

The result is a beautiful and mysterious story of grief and love, age and youth, politics and privacy. Nothing is simple and everything is radiant. The radiance comes from Thompson's clear intelligence, her vivid use of detail and her lyrical, expressive prose. I was struck by her ability to voice her characters' thoughts in a way that seems both appropriate for the period and timeless. Here is Edwin painting his sister-in-law just after he learns she is pregnant.

> *Upstairs in Samuel's sitting-room, Edwin paces before the canvas. A bowl of eggs on a table to the side of her .... He doesn't actually want a bowl of pristine pale eggs. In fact, he wants to remove the blue-and-white china vase from the sideboard and crack a single egg open in its place. What pleasure to paint its yolk vivid and yellow beside the orange of her. He begins to chuckle. The urge to juxtapose this with that irresistible. Might be trouble, egg yolk on mahogany. Probably make a bad stain.*

And here is Samuel's daughter closing a door: "Maud opens and closes the front door quietly, and the frame accepts the door in a complicit, silent embrace."

Over and over reading Thompson's prose I paused in admiration and then hurried on, longing to know where she would take

me next. And where she took me was an immensely satisfying destination, full of feeling as finally her characters embrace the present and sometimes, happily, each other. —*Margot Livesey*
Margot Livesey is fiction editor of Ploughshares. *Her latest novel is* The House on Fortune Street.

Eternal Enemies, *poems by Adam Zagajewski* (FSG): It sounds somewhat disingenuous now to call even a single poem beautiful, let alone an entire book, so it's not without caution that I say Adam Zagajewski's latest collection, *Eternal Enemies,* is exactly that: lovely, luminous, and wholly lacking the easy cynicism lesser poets might ascribe to such work. Its richness comes, in part, from Zagajewski's Polish heritage, and the war-savaged landscapes of his youth, which haunt his work even now, some thirty-six years after publishing his first book. Cities are of particular interest to Zagajewski, as places where lives intersect, or where history is measured against an individual life. The latter condition is explored in the opening poem, "Star," an ode to remembrance in which the poet returns to the "unchanging city / buried in the waters of the past." In many ways, it's the quintessential poem of the collection, clear-spoken yet complex. "I'm not," he says, "the young poet who wrote / too many lines // and wandered in the maze / of narrow streets and illusions." Many of Zagajewski's poems follow that mode of deceptive simplicity, where seemingly small associations lead to devastating conclusions. In "The Swallows of Auschwitz," the sound of birdcalls causes the poet to ask, "Is this really all that's left / of human speech?" Elsewhere, a Billie Holliday recording leads to a meditation on death and pain.

Even in poems without such historical burdens, Zagajewski reaches through the expected, finding the personal, for example, in a public discourse: "Yes, defending poetry, high style, etc. / but also summer evenings in a small town...." Of course, for a poet like Zagajewski, matters of art and matters of the self aren't far removed, and that tension becomes the driving force for several poems. It's fascinating to watch a poet of Zagajewski's stature grapple with such slippery subject matter as the natures of art or poetry. In one version, poetry is "the kingly road / that leads us farthest." In another, the act of reading poems becomes an elegy for the friends who wrote them. In this poem, the excellent "Butterflies," we see the perfect confluence of Zagajewski's poetic concerns, past and present uniting under the auspices of art, and offering his readers a guide of sorts to the stark, essential beauty he continues to give us: "I read poems, listen to the mighty whisper / of night and blood." —*Robert Arnold*

Robert Arnold is the managing director of Ploughshares, *and cofounder of* Memorious: a journal of new verse and fiction.

EDITORS' SHELF

Books Recommended by Our Advisory Editors

Robert Boswell recommends *Rare High Meadow of Which I Might Dream*, poems by Connie Voisine: "Connie Voisine's second book of poetry is a powerfully moving exploration of desire and the consequences of desire. The language has the clarity and precision of genius. A brilliant book." (Chicago)

Ron Carlson recommends *A Proper Knowledge*, a novel by Michelle Latiolais: "Here is a deep look at a doctor who works with autistic children, so frustrated with science and the tiny progress he's making with the young people with whom he works, that he comes to life himself. Latiolais writes sharply and beautifully about the interior of her characters." (Belleview Literary Press)

Jane Hirshfield recommends *The Opposite of Clairvoyance*, poems by Gillian Wegener: "This is a first collection of uncommonly sure-handed grace. These poems, many set in California's Central Valley, mix the recognizable with the revelatory in a way quietly but entirely Wegener's own. They see exactly what was there to be seen, but wasn't, and then they see a little more. This book's after-effect is expanded affection, increased reach." (Sixteen Rivers)

David St. John recommends *Litanies Near Water*, poems by Paula Clausson Buck: "Paula Clausson Buck's latest collection is a stunning and quietly elegant series of meditations upon the power of human endurance and the grace of the imagination. Sometimes these lyrics feel prayer-like in their simplicity, and timeless in their daily revelations." (LSU)

EDITORS' CORNER

New Books by Our Advisory Editors

Russell Banks, *The Reserve*, a novel: Part love story, part murder mystery, and set on the cusp of the Second World War, this deeply engaging new novel raises dangerous questions about class, politics, art, love, and madness. (Harper)

Charles Baxter, *The Soul Thief*, a novel: A graduate student is drawn into a tangle of relationships that cause him to question his own identity, in Baxter's compelling new novel. (Pantheon)

Frank Bidart, *Watching the Spring Festival*, poems: In these darkly radiant poems, mortality forces the self to question the relation between the life actually lived and what was once the promise of transformation. (FSG)

Mark Doty, *Fire to Fire*, new and selected poems: In this collection of the best from Doty's seven books, alongside a generous selection of new work, Doty's subjects echo and develop, his signature style encompassing both the plainspoken and the artfully wrought. (Harper)

Cornelius Eady, *Hardheaded Weather*, new and selected poems: This exciting new collection both delineates the arc of the poet's universe and highlights the range of his talents with sly, unsentimental, witty poems. (Marian Wood)

Jorie Graham, *Sea Change*, poems: Bringing readers to the threshold at which civilization becomes unsustainable, Graham questions how the human spirit might persist in a world where the future is no longer assured. (Ecco)

Edward Hirsch, *Special Orders*, poems: With a mixture of grief and joy, Hirsch assesses "the major triumphs, the major failures" of his life so far, revealing a new fearlessness in confronting his own internal divisions. (Knopf)

DeWitt Henry, *Safe Suicide,* essays: These interconnected essays tell the story of an ordinary man—a father of two, a husband, a long-time teacher and editor—and his extraordinary struggles for happiness and truth, offering moments of powerful insights and piercing revelations. (Red Hen Press)

Alice Hoffman, *The Third Angel*, a novel: Hoffman elegantly examines the lives of three women at different crossroads in their lives, tying their London-centered stories together in devastating retrospect. (Shaye Areheart)

Marie Howe, *The Kingdom of Ordinary Time*, poems: The speaker in this anticipated new volume of poems wonders: What is the difference between the self and the soul? The secular and the sacred? And how does one live in Ordinary Time—during those periods that are not apparently miraculous? (Norton)

Don Lee, *Wrack and Ruin*, a novel: Lee's second novel is an incisive satire about art and commerce, fame and ethnicity, nature and development, and two estranged brothers, Lyndon and Woody Song. (Norton)

Margot Livesey, *The House on Fortune Street*, a novel: This absorbing novel opens multiple perspectives on the life of Dara MacLeod, a young London therapist, partly by paying subtle homage to literary figures and works. (Harper)

Thomas Lux, *God Particles*, poems: A satiric edge cuts through many of the poems in this new collection, with unexpected moments of grace instilling even the darkest moments with surprising sweetness. (Houghton Mifflin)

Campbell McGrath, *Seven Notebooks*, poems: These seven poetic sequences examine—in forms ranging from haiku to prose, and in a voice veering from incantatory to deadpan—the world as it is seen, known, imagined, and dreamed. (Ecco)

Sue Miller, *The Senator's Wife*, a novel: In this rich, emotionally urgent novel, two women at opposite stages of life face parallel dilemmas. (Knopf)

Jay Neugeboren, *1940*, a novel: Neugeboren's first novel in twenty years presents a fictional account of an obscure historical figure, Dr. Eduard Bloch, an Austrian doctor who achieved notoriety for being Adolf Hitler's childhood physician. (Two Dollar Radio)

Charles Simic, *That Little Something*, poems: In his superb eighteenth collection, Simic moves closer to the dark heart of history and human behavior. (Harcourt)

Maura Stanton, *Immortal Sofa*, poems: In poems both humorous and elegaic, Maura Stanton gathers strange facts, odd events, and overlooked stories to construct her own vision of immortality. (Illinois)

Gerald Stern, *Save the Last Dance*, poems: Stern's latest is an intimate, yet always universal and surprising, book that's rich with humor and insight. (Norton)

Tobias Wolff, *Our Story Begins*, new and selected stories: The ten spare, elegant new stories, collected with twenty-one stories from Wolff's three previous collections, offer moments of realization, along with an expert use of irony and empathy to explore facets of contemporary life. (Knopf)

C. D. Wright, *Rising, Fall, Hovering*, poems: Wright's language is sharpened with political ferocity as she overlays voices from the borderlands between nations, to reveal the human struggle for connection and justice during times of upheaval and grief. (Copper Canyon)

CONTRIBUTORS' NOTES

Spring 2008

BETTY ADCOCK is the author of five books of poems, most recently *Intervale: New and Selected Poems*, finalist for the Lenore Marshall Prize and co-winner (with Caroline Kizer) of the 2003 Poets' Prize. Adcock has won two Pushcart Prizes, in addition to the North Carolina's Governor's Medal for Literature and the Texas Institute of Letters Prize. A 2002–2003 Guggenheim Fellow, she teaches at Meredith College and at the Warren Wilson M.F.A. Program for Writers.

WILLIAM BAER, a current Guggenheim fellow, is the author of fifteen books, including *The Ballad Rode into Town*, *Borges and Other Sonnets*, *Luís de Camões: Selected Sonnets*, *Writing Metrical Poetry*, and *Classic American Films: Conversations with the Screenwriters*.

CHRISTOPHER BAKKEN is the author of two books of poetry, *After Grace* and *Goat Funeral*, which won the Texas Institute of Letters Prize in 2006. He is also co-translator of *The Lion's Gate: Selected Poems of Titos Patrikios*.

GEORGE BILGERE directs the Creative Writing program at John Carroll University in Cleveland, Ohio. His recent books are *The Good Kiss* (Akron, 2002) and *Haywire* (Utah), which won the May Swenson Poetry Award in 2006. New poems are forthcoming in *Field* and *River Styx*.

MICHELLE BOISSEAU's third collection of poetry, *Trembling Air*, was published by the University of Arkansas Press and was a PEN USA finalist. New work has appeared in *Poetry*, *Kenyon Review*, *TriQuarterly*, *Shenandoah*, *Gettysburg Review*, and elsewhere. She directs the creative writing program at the University of Missouri—Kansas City. Her *Writing Poems* is in its seventh edition.

BRUCE BOND's collections of poetry include *Cinder*, *The Throats of Narcissus*, *Radiography*, *The Anteroom of Paradise*, *Independence Days*, and a new volume, *Blind Rain*, is forthcoming from LSU Press. His poetry has appeared in *Best American Poetry*, *The Yale Review*, *The Georgia Review*, *The Paris Review*, and elsewhere. He teaches at the University of North Texas, where he is Poetry Editor for *American Literary Review*.

ELIZABETH BRADFIELD is the author of *Interpretive Work* (Arktoi, 2008). Her poems about Antarctic exploration have appeared in *The Atlantic Monthly*, *Poetry*, *Field*, and elsewhere. She edits and manages Broadsided (www.broadsidedpress.org). Currently a Wallace Stegner Fellow, when not writing, she works as a naturalist and web designer.

JAMES BROWN is the author of several novels and *The Los Angeles Diaries: A Memoir*. His personal essays have appeared in *The New York Times Magazine*,

CONTRIBUTORS' NOTES

GQ, The Los Angeles Times Magazine, and *Best American Sports Writing of 2006.* He is also the recipient of an NEA fellowship for Fiction.

ROBERT CORDING teaches English and creative writing at College of the Holy Cross. He has published five collections of poems: *Life-list,* which won the Ohio State University Press/Journal award in 1987, *What Binds Us To This World, Heavy Grace, Against Consolation,* and, most recently, *Common Life.*

CHAD DAVIDSON is an associate professor of literature and creative writing at the University of West Georgia and the author of *Consolation Miracle.* His second book, *The Last Predicta,* will be published this year.

BARBARA DIMMICK lives near Rochester, NY, with her husband, some house cats, and a mischievous ghost. Her novels include *In the Presence of Horses* (Doubleday) and *Heart-Side Up* (Graywolf).

STEPHEN DUNN is the author of fourteen collections of poetry, including *Different Hours,* which was awarded the Pulitzer Prize. His Selected & New Poems: 1996–2008, entitled *What Goes On,* will be published by Norton in early 2009. He lives in Frostburg, Maryland.

PETER EVERWINE's most recent book of poems is *From the Meadow: Selected and New Poems.* A collection of his Aztec translations, *Working the Song Fields,* will be published in Spring 2009. He lives in Fresno, California.

GARY FINCKE's collection of poems, *Standing around the Heart,* was published in 2005 by the University of Arkansas Press, which will publish his next collection, *The Fire Landscape,* this fall. His collection of short stories, *Sorry I Worried You,* won the Flannery O'Connor Prize.

GREGORY FRASER is the author of *Strange Pietà* and *Answering the Ruins* , and co-author, with Chad Davidson, of *Poetry Writing: Creative-Critical Approaches.* The recipient of a grant from the NEA, he serves as associate professor of English at the University of West Georgia.

CAROL FROST is the author of ten collections of poems, most recently *I Will Say Beauty* (2003) and *The Queen's Desertion* (2006), both published by Northwestern University Press. The recipient of two fellowships from the National Endowment for the Arts and three Pushcart Prizes, Frost teaches at Hartwick College and directs the Catskill Poetry Workshop.

ALLEN GROSSMAN has published eleven books of poetry, most recently *Descartes' Loneliness* (New Directions, 2007). His critical work includes *The Sighted Singer* and a forthcoming collection, *True Love: Five Essays on Poetry.* The oak figuring in this poem grows near Lake of the Isles, in Minneapolis.

R. S. GWYNN is the editor of the Penguin Pocket Anthology series. Since 1976, he has taught at Lamar University, where he was recently named Distinguished Poet-in-Residence.

RACHEL HADAS is Board of Governors professor of English at the Newark campus of Rutgers University. The most recent of her many books are a poetry collection, *The River of Forgetfulness*, and a book of selected prose, *Classics*.

MARY STEWART HAMMOND's poems have appeared or are forthcoming in *The Atlantic Monthly, American Poetry Review, Boulevard, Gettysburg Review, Field, New Criterion, New England Review, The New Yorker, The Paris Review, Shenandoah, The Southern Review, The Yale Review*, and numerous anthologies. Her prize-winning book, *Out of Canaan*, was published by W.W. Norton.

SARAH HANNAH's poems have appeared or are forthcoming in *The Southern Review, Parnassus, Agni, Rattapallax, Western Humanities Review, New Millennium Writing, Michigan Quarterly Review, The Harvard Review*, and many other journals. She is the author of two collections, *Longing Distance* and *Inflorescence*, both published by Tupelo Press. Until her death in May 2007, Hannah taught poetry writing and literature at Emerson College.

C. G. HANZLICEK is the author of eight collections of poetry, most recently *The Cave: Selected and New Poems* (Pittsburgh, 2001).

BOB HICOK's most recent book is *This Clumsy Living* (Pittsburgh, 2007).

TONY HOAGLAND won the 2005 Mark Twain Award from the Poetry Foundation, for humor in American poetry. His books of poems include *What Narcissism Means to Me* and *Hard Rain*, and he's also the author of *Real Sofitikashun*, a book of essays on craft (2006). He teaches at the University of Houston and in the Warren Wilson M.F.A. program.

CHRISTIE HODGEN is the author of the novel, *Hello, I Must Be Going*, and the story collection, *A Jeweler's Eye for Flaw*. She lives in Kansas City.

COLETTE INEZ has published nine books of poetry and has won Guggenheim, Rockefeller, and two NEA fellowships and Pushcart Prizes. She is widely anthologized and teaches in Columbia University's Undergraduate Writing Program. Her memoir, *The Secret of M. Dulong*, was recently released by The University of Wisconsin Press.

ROY JACOBSTEIN was a finalist for The Academy of American Poets' Walt Whitman Prize for his latest book, *Ripe*, which won the Felix Pollak Prize. His next three books of poetry are currently seeking homes. Working internationally as a public health physician on women's reproductive health, he divides his time between Chapel Hill, Addis Ababa, Phnom Penh, New York, and Lilongwe.

MARK JARMAN's most recent collections of poetry include *Epistles, To the Green Man, Unholy Sonnets*, and *Questions for Ecclesiastes*, which won the 1998 Lenore Marshall Poetry Prize and was a finalist for the National Book Critics Circle Award. He is Centennial Professor of English at Vanderbilt University.

TED KOOSER served as U. S. Poet Laureate in 2004–2006 and won the Pulitzer Prize in poetry for his book, *Delights & Shadows*, in 2005. He lives in rural Nebraska and teaches poetry and essay writing part time at The University of

Nebraska. His most recent book is *Valentines* (Nebraska), which is a collection of his annual valentine poems written over the past twenty-two years.

JEFFREY LEVINE is the author of *Mortal, Everlasting*, which won the 2001 Transcontinental Poetry Award from Pavement Saw Press. Among other distinctions, he has won the Larry Levis Poetry Prize from the Missouri Review, the Kestral Prize, the first annual James Hearst Poetry Award from *North American Review*, and the *Mississippi Review* Prize. He is Editor-in-Chief of Tupelo Press.

WILLIAM LYCHACK is the author of a novel, *The Wasp Eater*, and a forthcoming collection of stories, *The Architect of Flowers*. He is the writer-in-residence at Phillips Academy.

DAVID MASON's books include *The Country I Remember, Arrivals*, and the verse novel *Ludlow*. He has edited several anthologies, and his work appears in such magazines as *Poetry, TLS, Harper's, The Nation, The New Republic*, and *The Hudson Review*. He teaches at The Colorado College.

MAILE MELOY is the author of the story collection *Half in Love* and the novels *Liars and Saints* and *A Family Daughter*. Her new collection of short stories will be published next year.

MICHAEL MEYERHOFER's first book, *Leaving Iowa*, won the Liam Rector First Book Award. He also published four chapbooks and recently received the James Wright Poetry Award. His work has appeared or is forthcoming in *River Styx, Arts & Letters, North American Review, Green Mountains Review*, and others.

ROBERT MEZEY is the recipient of awards from the American Academy of Arts and Letters, PEN, the Ingram Merrill and Guggenheim Foundations, and the NEA, among other distinctions. His books include *The Lovermaker, A Book of Dying, White Blossoms, The Door Standing Open, Small Song, Couplets, Selected Translations, Evening Wind*, and *Collected Poems 1952–1999*.

D. NURKSE's recent books of poetry include *The Fall, Burnt Island*, and *The Border Kingdom*. He received a 2007 Guggenheim Fellowship, and teaches at Sarah Lawrence College.

ALICIA OSTRIKER's most recent books of poetry are *The Volcano Sequence* and *No Heaven*. Her most recent prose works are *Dancing at the Devil's Party: Essays on Poetry, Politics and the Erotic* and *For the Love of God: the Bible as an Open Book*. She lives in Princeton, New Jersey.

ALISON PELEGRIN is the author of *Big Muddy River of Stars* (Akron, 2007), *The Zydeco Tablets* (Word, 2002), and three prize-winning chapbooks, the most recent of which is *Squeezers* (Concrete Wolf, 2005). She is the recipient of fellowships from the Louisiana Division of the Arts, and the NEA.

CATHERINE PIERCE is the author of *Famous Last Words*, winner of the 2007 Saturnalia Books Poetry Prize, as well as of a chapbook, *Animals of Habit* (Kent State, 2004). Recent work has appeared in *Slate, Gulf Coast, Blackbird, Best New Poets 2007*, and elsewhere. She teaches at Mississippi State University.

RON RASH is the author of three poetry collections and six books of fiction. His latest novel, *Serena*, will be published by Ecco in September of this year. He teaches at Western Carolina University.

JAY ROGOFF's third book of poems, *The Long Fault*, has just appeared from LSU Press. He has also published *The Cutoff* and *How We Came to Stand on That Shore*, and has newer poems in *AGNI*, *Literary Imagination*, *Salmagundi*, and other journals. He lives in Saratoga Springs, New York.

CLARE ROSSINI's second full-length collection, *Lingo*, was published by the University of Akron Press in 2006. Her poems have appeared widely, in anthologies such as *Poets for the New Century* and the *Best American Poetry* series. She teaches at Trinity College and in the Vermont College M.F.A. Program.

GERALD SHAPIRO is the author of three collections of stories and novellas: *From Hunger*, *Bad Jews and Other Stories*, and *Little Men*. His fiction and nonfiction have appeared in *Witness*, *Gettysburg Review*, *Southern Review*, *Ploughshares*, *Kenyon Review*, *Missouri Review*, and many other journals. He teaches creative writing and literature at the University of Nebraska-Lincoln.

FAITH SHEARIN's first book, *The Owl Question*, won the May Swenson Award. A second, *The Empty House*, is forthcoming from Word Press in 2008. Recent poems appear in *North American Review* and *Sweeping Beauty: an anthology of female poets*. She lives with her husband and daughter in North Carolina.

MAURYA SIMON has published seven poetry volumes, including *Ghost Orchid*, nominated for a 2004 National Book Award. Her new volume, *Cartographies*, is forthcoming in 2008. Simon has received fellowships from the NEA, Fulbright Foundation, and American Academy in Rome. She teaches at the University of California, Riverside.

JULIE SUK is the author of four poetry collections, most recently *The Dark Takes Aim* (Autumn House). She has been a recipient of the Bess Hokin Prize from *Poetry* magazine, and has work forthcoming in *Shenandoah* and *Triquarterly*.

ANNE-MARIE THOMPSON graduated from Texas Christian University in 2005 with a degree in Piano Performance. She currently resides in Fort Worth, Texas, where she teaches piano and gives lecture-recitals.

DAVID TUCKER won the 2005 Bakeless prize for poetry, selected by Philip Levine. The book, *Late for Work*, was published by Houghton Mifflin. He is deputy managing editor at the *New Jersey Star-Ledger*. Last year, he was awarded a Witter Bynner fellowship from the Library of Congress, selected by Poet Laureate Donald Hall.

CHARLES HARPER WEBB's book, *Amplified Dog*, won the Saltman Prize for Poetry and was published in 2006 by Red Hen Press. His book of prose poems, *Hot Popsicles*, was published in 2005 by the University of Wisconsin Press. Recipient of grants from the Whiting and Guggenheim foundations, he directs Creative Writing at California State University, Long Beach.

ALEXIS WIGGINS's work has appeared in *Creative Nonfiction, Story South, Brevity, Ruminator*, W. W. Norton's anthology *Best Creative Nonfiction Volume 1* (2007), and was nominated for a Pushcart Prize in 2004. She divides her time between New York and Madrid.

ALAN WILLIAMSON's most recent books are *The Pattern More Complicated: New and Selected Poems* (Chicago) and *Westernness: A Meditation* (Virginia). He teaches at the University of California at Davis and in the Warren Wilson M.F.A. Program for Writers.

IRENE WILLIS has published two poetry collections, *They Tell Me You Danced* (Florida) and *At the Fortune Cafe*, which was awarded the 2005 Violet Reed Haas Poetry Prize by Snake Nation Press. Her new manuscript, *Those Flames*, is seeking a publisher.

∼

GUEST EDITOR POLICY *Ploughshares* is published three times a year: mixed issues of poetry and fiction in the Spring and Winter and a fiction issue in the Fall, with each guest-edited by a different writer of prominence, usually one whose early work was published in the journal. Guest editors are invited to solicit up to half of their issues, with the other half selected from unsolicited manuscripts screened for them by staff editors. This guest editor policy is designed to introduce readers to different literary circles and tastes, and to offer a fuller representation of the range and diversity of contemporary letters than would be possible with a single editorship. Yet, at the same time, we expect every issue to reflect our overall standards of literary excellence. We liken *Ploughshares* to a theater company: each issue might have a different guest editor and different writers—just as a play will have a different director, playwright, and cast—but subscribers can count on a governing aesthetic, a consistency in literary values and quality, that is uniquely our own.

∼

SUBMISSION POLICIES We welcome unsolicited manuscripts from August 1 to March 31 (postmark dates). All submissions sent from April to July are returned unread. In the past, guest editors often announced specific themes for issues, but we have revised our editorial policies and no longer restrict submissions to thematic topics. Submit your work at any time during our reading period; if a manuscript is not timely for one issue, it will be considered for another. We do not recommend trying to target specific guest editors. Our backlog is unpredictable, and staff editors ultimately have the responsibility of determining for which editor a work is most appropriate. Mail one prose piece or one to three poems. We do not accept e-mail submissions, but we plan to introduce an online submissions system this fall. Check for updates and guidelines on our website (www.pshares.org). Poems should be individually typed either single- or double-spaced on one side of the page. Prose should be typed double-spaced on one side and be no longer than thirty pages. Although we look primarily for short stories, we occasionally publish personal essays/memoirs. Novel excerpts are acceptable if self-contained. Unsolicited book reviews and criticism are not considered. Please do not send multiple submissions of the same genre, and do not send another manuscript until you hear about the first. *No more than a total of two submissions per reading period.* Additional submissions will be returned unread. Mail your manuscript in a page-size manila envelope, your full name and address written on the outside. In general, address submissions to the "Fiction Editor," "Poetry Editor," or "Nonfiction Editor," not to the guest or staff editors by name, unless you have a legitimate association with them or have been previously published in the magazine. Unsolicited work sent directly to a guest editor's home or office will be ignored and discarded; guest editors are formally instructed not to read such work. *All manuscripts and correspondence regarding submissions should be accompanied by a business-size, self-addressed, stamped envelope (s.a.s.e.) for a response only. Manuscript copies will be recycled, not returned.* No replies will be given by postcard or e-mail (exceptions are made for international submissions). Expect three to five months for a decision. We now receive well over a thousand manuscripts a month. Do not query us until five months have passed, and if you do, please write to us, including an s.a.s.e. and indicating the postmark date of submission, instead of calling or e-mailing. Simultaneous submissions are amenable as long as they are indicated as such and we are notified immediately upon acceptance elsewhere. We cannot accommodate revisions, changes of return address, or forgotten s.a.s.e.'s after the fact. We do not reprint previously published work. Translations are welcome if permission has been granted. We cannot be responsible for delay, loss, or damage. Payment is upon publication: $25/printed page, $50 minimum and $250 maximum per author, with two copies of the issue and a one-year subscription.

Live in Words

Master of Fine Arts in
Creative Writing
Concentrations in Fiction, Poetry, and Nonfiction

Master of Arts in
Publishing & Writing
Concentrations in Book, Magazine, and Electronic Publishing

Creative Writing Faculty
Jonathan Aaron
Ben Brooks
Christine Casson
Maria Flook
Lise Haines
DeWitt Henry
Richard Hoffman
Bill Knott
Margot Livesey
Megan Marshall
Gail Mazur
Kim McLarin
William Orem
Pamela Painter
Jon Papernick
Frederick Reiken
John Skoyles
Daniel Tobin, Chair
Jessica Treadway
Douglas Whynott
Mako Yoshikawa

Publishing Faculty
Bill Beuttler
Lisa Diercks
David Emblidge
Gian Lombardo
Jeffrey Seglin
Daniel Weaver

Emerson College offers a thriving community of diverse writers and aspiring leaders in the publishing industry. Defined by close collaboration and support from award-winning faculty mentors and fellow students, our Programs connect Emerson students to Boston's distinguished literary tradition. In addition, students have the opportunity to teach and hold internships in nationally known magazines and presses.

Our graduates have published with major publishing houses, started their own journals and presses, and assumed editorial and design positions within the industry. Other alumni accomplishments include the Pushcart Prize, AWP Intro Award, Grolier Poetry Prize and Fulbright, Stegner, Bunting Institute, FAWC, and Ruth Lilly Poetry fellowships.

Presidential and Merit Aid scholarships are available.

EMERSON COLLEGE
BOSTON MASSACHUSETTS

Emerson College
Office of Graduate Admission
120 Boylston Street
Boston, Massachusetts
02116-4624

www.emerson.edu
gradapp@emerson.edu
617-824-8610

All good writing is swimming underwater and holding your breath. — F. Scott Fitzgerald

James A. Michener Center for Writers **MFA IN WRITING**
Fiction • Poetry • Screenwriting • Playwriting

Upcoming and recent faculty
ANTONYA NELSON
ZZ PACKER
DEAN YOUNG
COLM TOIBIN
ANTHONY GIARDINA
AUGUST KLEINZAHLER
JOHN DUFRESNE
JOY WILLIAMS
DENIS JOHNSON
MARIE HOWE

Fellowships of $25,000 annually for three years
512/471.1601 • www.utexas.edu/academic/mcw

THE UNIVERSITY OF TEXAS AT AUSTIN